Campus Cravings:
Dorm Life

Total-E-Bound Publishing books in print from
Carol Lynne:

Campus Cravings Volume One: On the Field
Coach
Side-Lined
Sacking the Quarterback

Campus Cravings Volume Two: Off the Field
Off Season
Forbidden Freshman

Campus Cravings Volume Three: Back on Campus
Broken Pottery
In Bear's Bed

Campus Cravings Volume Four: Dorm Life
Office Advances
A Biker's Vow

Good-Time Boys
Sonny's Salvation
Garron's Gift
Rawley's Redemption
Twin Temptations

Cattle Valley Volume One
All Play & No Work
Cattle Valley Mistletoe

Cattle Valley Volume Two
Sweet Topping
Rough Ride

Campus Cravings
Volume Four

DORM LIFE

Office Advances

A Biker's Vow

CAROL LYNNE

Campus Cravings: Dorm Life
ISBN # 978-1-906590-31-4
©Copyright Carol Lynne 2008
Cover Art by Lyn Taylor ©Copyright 2008
Interior text design by Claire Siemaszkiewicz
Total-E-Bound Publishing

Published in 2008 by Total-E-Bound Publishing Faldingworth Road, Spridlington, Market Rasen, Lincolnshire, LN8 2DE, UK.
No part of this book may be reproduced, scanned, or distributed in any printed or electronic form without permission. Please do not participate in or encourage piracy of copyrighted materials in violation of the authors' rights. Purchase only authorised copies.
Total-E-Bound Publishing is an imprint of
Total-E-Ntwined Limited.

Manufactured in the USA.

OFFICE
ADVANCES

Dedication

For Drew Hunt

Chapter One

"Have you seen Sam?" Tony Bianchi asked.

Charlie looked towards Tony and shook his head, "So not funny."

"Sorry," Tony walked into the common room at BK House and sat on the couch. "Liam said he might be interested in a part-time job."

"He's in the computer room, I think." Charlie said, munching on another handful of popcorn.

"What's wrong with the one in his room?" Tony asked. He tried to sneak a few kernels from Charlie's bowl but he got his hand slapped.

"Ask."

Tony rolled his eyes. "Can I please have some of your popcorn?"

Charlie grinned and passed the bowl over. "See that wasn't so hard. And there's nothing wrong with Sam's computer. His roommate, Lark Wilsher, is meditating. He does it every evening at this time. Something about cleansing the negativity he gathers during the day." Charlie shrugged like he didn't believe in any of it.

"Whatever floats his boat," Tony said, handing the bowl back.

"Thanks, I'll stick my head back in before I take off," Tony said as he rose off the couch.

Tony found Sam right where Charlie said he'd be. He knocked on the glass door before entering. "Okay if I interrupt?"

"Mr. Bianchi," Sam said. He saved his work to a jump drive and turned in his chair to face Tony.

"I won't take up much of your time. I was talking to Liam earlier and he said you might be interested in a part-time job."

"Sure, would I be doing the same thing Liam does for you?"

"Not exactly. I need someone on site for a few hours a day. I've acquired a new company and their files are a mess. I need someone to go through and scan the appropriate documents into the computer. Sorry to say it's a boring job, but it'll pay more than you can make working part-time anywhere else."

Sam seemed to hesitate momentarily. "Who would I be working for?"

"Me," Tony replied.

"I'm out of classes by two. Would that give me enough time?"

"Yeah, it should. If you can get there by two-thirty it'll give you three and a half hours a day. So can I count on you?" Tony stuck his hand out.

Standing, Sam nodded and shook Tony's hand. "Thanks, Mr. Bianchi. I won't let you down."

"Tony, please. Can you start this week?"

"Yeah, that would be perfect. We're out of class this week for Spring Break."

Shaking his head, Tony chuckled. "I should know that. Hell, I live with a teacher. But in my own defence, Daniel works five days a week regardless if class is in session or not. Why aren't you taking off like most of the college kids?"

Sam grinned and pulled out his empty pockets. "It's the reason I need a job."

"Come in any time. You can work as many hours as you have time for until classes start up again."

"Thank you, Mr... Tony."

Tony shook Sam's hand again and thumped him on the back. "Good to have you on board. Come see me when you get there."

"I will," Sam said, with a wide grin plastered to his face.

* * * *

The next morning, Sam took extra time with his hair, but his unruly curls refused to be tamed. He wondered if he should get it cut. Giving up, he found an elastic band and pulled it back at the nape of his neck. At least from the front he'd look somewhat professional.

Looking at his shirt, he tried to smooth out the wrinkles. "Who am I kidding? I'll never fit in."

"Who're you talking to?" Bear asked walking into the communal bathroom.

"Myself," Sam answered. "I start at Bianchi Bytes in an hour. I couldn't look any less like a corporate employee if I tried."

Bear smiled and pulled the end of Sam's short ponytail. "You'll be fine. Tony wouldn't have offered you the job if he was worried about you fitting in."

Sam shrugged. "I guess so." He took one last look at himself and dug some gunk out of the corner of his eye. "Wish me luck."

"You don't need it," Bear replied, dropping his towel and stepping into the shower.

Blushing, Sam quickly looked away. "I'll see you later at dinner."

"Bye," Bear called out.

Sam ran down the steps and down to the corner. He hoped the busses were running on time. He had to transfer at Jacobs Street, but it shouldn't be that long of a ride. He'd plotted it all out on the computer after Tony had left the previous evening.

He still couldn't believe he would be working in the same building with Jace Rawlings. Hopefully they wouldn't run into each other much. He doubted he'd ever feel comfortable around Jace again.

The bus pulled up to the curb and Sam hopped on, depositing his money before finding a seat. He knew he hadn't been crazy. Jace had definitely been giving off attraction vibes in the car the day they went to find Bear.

While they waited for Liam to retrieve his wayward boyfriend, they'd finally started talking. Then he did it. He had actually asked Jace out. The reaction he received had been like a slap in the face.

Sam still remembered Jace's words exactly. "I don't date kids."

Hell, Sam hadn't thought of himself as a kid since he was thirteen. Being the man of the family, he'd gotten a job at the age of fourteen. It may have been back breaking manual labour working at the grain mill, but it helped pay the bills.

Jace was what, around thirty-six, thirty-seven? Older yes, but in no way was he too old for Sam. Thoughts of that day had Sam completely depressed as he pushed open the door of the glass office building.

Walking up to the information counter, Sam gave the woman his name and asked for Tony. She smiled and pointed towards the bank of elevators. "Mr. Bianchi is expecting you. His office is on the fourth floor. Turn to your right and you'll find him."

Sam thanked her and stood in line with a group of people in front of the elevator. It seemed to take forever for the doors to open. He made a mental note to take the stairs in the future. Although his knee was too shot to play soccer, he could still make it up four flights. Maybe he'd get lucky and would be working on a lower floor.

As the elevator stopped at the individual floors, people trickled off to their day of work. Sam wiped his hands on his khaki trousers. He was a little surprised by the apparent dress code. Unlike most offices he'd been in, this one appeared a lot more casual. That was a good thing because he only owned a single pair of khaki's and a couple of button-up shirts.

The ding announced his arrival on the fourth floor. Taking a deep breath, Sam stepped out and made a right hand turn and ran into a solid wall of muscle. Surprised, he jerked back. Two strong arms reached out and caught him before he could do something totally embarrassing, like falling.

He didn't need to look up to know who had a hold of him.

"What're you doing here?" Jace asked, releasing his grip on Sam's arms.

Sam's mouth went dry as dirt. Shit. "Tony hired me to work part-time," he managed to get out.

"I was just in his office and he didn't mention it."

Sam shrugged his shoulders. "Sorry."

Jace crossed his arms, causing the material over his chest to strain at the seams. Sam averted his eyes. Don't look. Do not look. When Jace didn't say anything more, Sam chanced a quick glance at his face. He was met by a pair of the prettiest brown eyes in the world.

It looked like Jace wanted to say something, but instead gave his head a slight shake and walked around Sam without a word. Great, it was his first day and he'd already had a run-in with the object of his fantasies. It didn't help that Jace was the Vice-President of Bianchi Bytes.

Sam turned and watched Jace enter an office and shut the door. Closing his eyes, Sam sent up a quick prayer that he wouldn't be working on the fourth floor.

* * * *

It was the end of the day before he knew it. Sam had gotten his wish. He was about as far away from Jace as he could get and still be in the same building. Ensconced in a windowless supply closet on the first floor, Sam had spent the day organising. If he was going to spend his time in here, it needed to feel less cluttered.

Tony had ordered a small desk and the necessary computer equipment be brought to him which had arrived about an hour after he did. The boxes piled around were his first order of business. Getting a permanent marker from the supply clerk, he started thumbing through the boxes, marking dates on the outside. After they were all labelled with the appropriate dates, he organised them into groups.

After setting his last cardboard monstrosity into place, Sam stood back and surveyed his work. He had a lot more room and was eager to get started the next day. He decided he enjoyed the feeling of accomplishment after a job well done.

He felt a little lighter as he pulled on his jacket and picked up his lunch bag. Sam dug the small piece of paper out of his pocket and stuck it into his billfold. His 'new office' had a security lock and he'd need the combination to get back in. Once the code was tucked safely in his hip pocket, Sam pulled open the door and turned off the lights.

He was rounding the corner when he spotted Jace stepping off the elevator. Phone to his ear, Jace was laughing like he didn't have a care in the world. Sam wished he knew who could make the six-foot-one-inch man smile like that.

In a split second, Sam's mood went from up to down. Not wanting to be seen, Sam sighed and stepped back around the corner. He counted to one hundred before re-emerging into the lobby.

With a heavy heart, he walked to his bus stop, crumpled brown bag in his hand.

Chapter Two

"Mr. Bianchi would like to see you in his office," the woman at the information desk told him two mornings later as he passed.

"Oh, okay," Sam said. He veered off course and headed towards the stairs. He was half-way up before he realised he should have put his lunch in his office first. Oh well, too late now. By the time he got to the fourth floor his knee was starting to hurt. He stopped just inside the hallway and bent over to run his hand over the swollen joint.

"Problem?"

Sam's hand stilled. Standing upright he looked into those dark chocolate eyes of his dreams. "No."

Jace gestured to Sam's leg. "Did you hurt yourself?"

Sam shook his head and clutched his sack lunch in his fist. "It's an old injury. I guess I should've taken the elevator instead of the stairs."

Jace looked him up and down. He felt Jace's gaze like a caress against his skin. What the fuck? "The stairs are better for you. Just take them slow," Jace said in that deep whiskey voice that Sam loved.

"Uh, yeah, thanks."

Jace gave him one last look before turning and walking away. Sam exhaled and leaned back against the steel fire door. God he hoped Jace hadn't noticed the rising bulge in his khaki's.

Once his body was back under control, Sam headed for Tony's office. To his surprise the door was open. Sam knocked on the door jam. "You wanted to see me?" He hoped he wasn't being fired so soon. He really needed the money. His sleep had suffered since taking the job, but that wasn't Tony's fault. It was Jace's. Damn him and that sexy voice and body.

"Come in," Tony said, rising to greet him, before sitting back down.

Sam took a seat in one of the expensive-looking chairs in front of Tony's desk.

Tony rested on his forearms and studied Sam for a few seconds. "I have a favour to ask."

Sam's eyes rounded. The boss was asking him for a favour? "Okay," he said.

"Don't agree until I tell you what it is," he grinned.

"Okay."

"The company we bought found another storage facility for files. I'm sending Jace down to Florida to help deal with the transfer, but I'd like to send you as well. I think you've gone over the files enough to know if the boxes contain useful information, or if they are simply garbage. I don't really want to ship an entire truckload of boxes only to find out they are useless."

Sam felt his stomach drop. "Uh, have you talked to Jace about this?"

"Not yet, why?"

"Well, he may not want to have me tagging along. I'd be more than happy to help you out, but I'd prefer you speak to him before I give you a definite answer."

Tony seemed a little surprised. "There shouldn't be any problem. Jace gets along with everyone."

"Except me," Sam mumbled too low for Tony to hear.

"Still, I'll talk to him and let you know in a couple of hours. I'd like to see the two of you fly out this evening. That way you can get an early start in the morning and be back in town before classes resume on Monday." Tony stood indicating the meeting was over.

Sam picked his brown lunch sack up from the floor. "Thank you for asking me."

Tony clapped Sam on the back. "I'll let you know as soon as I can."

* * * *

Jace had just ended a call when his secretary's voice sounded over the intercom. "Tony called while you were on the phone. He'd like to see you in his office."

"Thanks, Janet." Jace stretched and looked out the window. His life had been turned upside down lately, and it was starting to affect his body. He needed to get back into the pool.

As he walked out of his office, he stopped by Janet's desk. "Is there a health club in town with a pool?"

Janet shook her head. "There's a pool at the college, but that and the pool at the Windsor Hotel are the only indoor pools I know of."

"Thanks," he said, walking towards Tony's office.

Maybe it would be worth the money to spend the night at the hotel? Until he'd moved to Idaho, he'd swim daily in his backyard. Maybe the college had an open swim.

With a knock, Jace entered Tony's office. "Can you do me a favour and ask Daniel if the college has open swim times?"

"Sure," Tony said. "Maybe you could swim in the ocean. How about a trip to Florida?"

The thought of once again swimming in the strong waves of the ocean was a dream come true. "Sure, what have you got for me?"

"I need you to go down to Miami. Phil Johnson called to tell me they found another storage unit full of old files. I'd like to send you and Sam Howard down to look them over."

"What? Why would you send Sam?" Jace felt his palms begin to sweat.

"He's the one who's been scanning the files. He's already organised our existing boxes. I thought he'd be the best person to send, but I don't want to send him alone. Why? Do you have a problem with him?"

Shit. Jace didn't know what to say. Hell yes I have a problem with him. I can't seem to keep my mind off his ass. "No. No problem. Separate rooms though, right?"

Tony looked confused. "Of course, when have I ever made employees bunk up?"

"Just checking," Jace said.

Tony tilted his head to the side and narrowed his eyes. "Is there something going on between you and Sam? I already spoke to him earlier and he said to ask him again after I'd talked to you."

Jace exhaled and slumped into a chair. "He asked me out and I made a fool of myself."

"Oh?"

"I told him I didn't date kids." Jace ran his fingers through his hair.

"I would hardly call Sam a kid. What's the real problem?"

Jace shrugged. "I just can't do it. I've got too much on my plate as it is." He didn't like discussing his private life, even with one of his best friends.

"Kade?"

"Yeah."

"I know you well enough to leave that subject alone. Just tell me you'll do this for me?"

"Sure," Jace sighed. "When do you need us there?"

"There's a flight to Miami leaving at four. That should put you in early enough to get a decent night's sleep. I told Phil you'd meet him in the morning in the hotel lobby around eight."

Jace looked at his watch. "Okay, I'll finish a few things up around here before going home to pack. Tell Sam I'll pick him up at BK at one-thirty. That should give us plenty of time to get to the airport and check in."

"Thanks, Jace."

* * * *

"Hey, watcha doing?" Liam asked sticking his head in Sam's room.

"Packing," Sam answered throwing another shirt in the duffle bag. "Tony's sending me to Miami for a few days to look at some files."

"Wow, cool." Liam came into the room and flopped on Sam's bed.

"No, not so cool." Sam turned from his small closet and looked at his friend. "He's sending Jace down with me."

"Ooh, ouch."

"Yeah." Sam picked a shirt up from the floor and smelled it, wondering if it was clean enough to take.

"So are you going to take advantage of the situation?"

"What? No. Jace humiliated me once. I'm not about to stick my neck out again. Hey, do you have a dress shirt I can borrow?"

"Not really. Maybe you should call Aaron? I bet he's got something."

"I don't really have time. Jace is coming at one-thirty." Sam pulled a black golf shirt out of the closet. "Will this do?"

"Sure." Liam studied the contents of the duffle for a few moments. "What, no trunks?"

"Nope. I don't own any. Back home if I wanted to swim in the pond, I just wore cut-offs."

They heard Bear calling down the hall for his boyfriend. Liam rolled his eyes and stood. "Better go see what he wants. Good luck on your trip. Try and enjoy yourself. Who knows when you'll ever get to Miami again."

"Yeah, thanks. See you Sunday evening."

Liam waved as he walked out the door. Sam looked at his duffle. Liam was right. Why shouldn't he enjoy himself? He was a young, good-looking guy. Surely he could hook-up with someone while in Florida.

He walked out of his room to the bathroom. One thing BK House had in plenty of supply was condoms. He took a handful out of the box on the counter. Might as well be prepared.

Chapter Three

Closing his hotel room door, Sam set his duffle on the bed. Wow, that had been awkward. The entire ride to the airport, waiting for the plane, and then the flight over had been done in relative silence.

Even though he and Jace sat so close on the plane their thighs had rubbed against one another, nothing. Jace hadn't so much as said boo to him. As soon as the seatbelt sign had gone off, Jace had pulled out his laptop and buried himself in work.

With their close proximity, Sam had been forced to call the flight attendant for a blanket to cover his rising erection. At least Jace hadn't seemed to notice his predicament.

They'd parted in the hallway, as Jace took the first room and Sam the second. Now, looking around, he knew he couldn't just go to bed. If he did, he'd think of nothing but Jace. He decided it was time to go down to a club and see who was still up. Who knew, maybe Mr. Right was sitting at the bar waiting for him.

He reached over and picked up the phone to call the front desk. He was told there was a gay club only about three blocks away. At the thought of getting lucky, Sam decided to step into the shower for a quick wash. He ran his hands down his chest to the cropped nest of hair surrounding his cock. He was so tempted to alleviate the ache, but he knew if he did, he'd be ready for bed before scouting the bar.

Soaping his hands, Sam quickly washed, only spending a few delicious minutes on his puckered hole. Stepping out, he reached for his kit and took out the lube. He had always made it a practice to wear a small plug whenever he went trolling. Better to be prepared than suffer a painful fucking in the bathroom.

He lifted his foot to the top of the toilet as he lubed and inserted the small, four inch lavender plug. His aim wasn't to get off, simply to be prepared.

Leaving his long curls to fall to the top of his shoulders, he dressed in a pair of jeans and tight white T-shirt. He splashed on a little of the cologne his mom had bought him for Christmas. As he sat on the edge of the bed to slip his athletic shoes on, he felt the plug shift.

A moan escaped his lips as he shifted again. Shoes tied, Sam stood and looked at himself in the mirror. He couldn't help but notice the bulge behind his fly. Good, maybe that would get him the attention he desired. Grabbing his key card and wallet from the nightstand, Sam left the room.

The ride down from the third floor to the lobby took mere seconds and Sam was ready. He pushed through the hotel door and took a left. He spotted the sign that read Pinky's, and stepped inside. Making his way to the bar, he grinned at the attention he was already receiving. *Oh yeah, he was going to get lucky tonight.*

For a weeknight, the place was packed. There must be a lot of vacationers this time of year. Straddling the closest bar stool he could find, Sam held up his hand for a drink. The hard wooden stool seemed to push the plug deeper into his already sensitive body and Sam had to bite his lip to stifle the moan.

"Can I help you?" the stud behind the bar asked.

"Sure, give me a beer and whatever else you'd like." God, look at him already flirting shamelessly.

The bartender smiled and filled a frosty glass from the tap.

Sam pulled out a ten and passed it across the smooth wooden surface. "Busy place," he said over the music.

The bartender rang up the sale, counted out the appropriate change and passed it back. He leaned forward and spoke into Sam's ear. "Half-price drink specials. Brings them in every time," he pulled back and winked at Sam.

"Cool," Sam said. He left the change on the bar as he took a drink.

Within moments, a tall good-looking man approached him. "Care to dance?"

Sam held up his finger and finished off his beer. One thing he'd learned was to never leave your drink unattended. He stood and shoved the bills into his front pocket. "I'm Sam," he said.

"Bob," the blond man replied.

Wrapping his arm around Sam's waist, Bob led him to the dance floor. It was one of the faster dance mixes, so there weren't as many people on the floor as there had been when Sam had walked in.

He had only started to dance, when Bob pulled him against his much larger frame. With a slight smile, Sam tried to put a little distance between them. He wanted to get lucky, but he didn't much care for getting mauled.

Bob's hands landed on Sam's ass and pulled him in once more. This time, Bob took advantage of their close proximity to grind himself against Sam. "Whoa there, Bob," Sam said in the man's ear. "Let's get to know each other a little first."

"What's there to know? I plan on fucking you into the wall later. That's all you need to know."

Something about the way Bob said it sent up warning signals. Sam tried to pull away. "Sorry, Bob, but I think I've made a mistake."

Bob grabbed his arms and tried to pull him back in. Sam shook his head. "Stop it. Leave me the fuck alone."

He was so busy struggling with the big brute he didn't notice the body behind him. "Problem?"

Sam looked over his shoulder at Jace. Even though it was a little humiliating, Sam nodded. "This asshole won't let me go."

Jace looked from Sam to Bob. He stepped around Sam to put a hand on Bob's shoulder. "Sorry, pal, but my friend came to Miami with me and he's leaving with me." Jace looked back at Sam. "Right now," he ground out between clenched jaws.

"You weren't with him a few minutes ago."

"My mistake, now please remove your hands."

Bob studied Jace for a few moments. "Fuck off," he said.

Jace started to walk away before turning back around and landing a right hook to the middle of Bob's perfect face. Bob immediately tried to cover his bleeding nose.

"You bastard! You broke my fucking nose."

Jace shrugged and pulled Sam towards the door, with Bob yelling obscenities at them the entire walk out. Once they were on the sidewalk, Jace released Sam and stalked towards the hotel.

"Of all the stupid, juvenile..." Jace stopped mid-stride and turned to face Sam. "What the hell were you thinking going out alone?" He didn't wait for an answer before he turned back around and started walking again, his long legs eating up the sidewalk.

Sam knew better than to say anything. He kept his head down and followed Jace to their hotel. Shit, he only hoped this didn't get him fired.

When they walked into the hotel, Sam headed for the stairs. No way in hell did he want to ride up with Jace.

"Where are you going?" Jace asked, hands on his hips. The elevator doors opened and Jace motioned to them. "Get in."

With his head up, Sam got in the elevator. As soon as the doors closed, Jace had him pushed against the wall, his mouth on Sam's. Jace slid his tongue into Sam's mouth at his surprised gasp.

Sam closed his eyes and savoured the taste of whiskey on Jace's tongue. Jace insinuated his thigh between Sam's spread legs and applied pressure to his rock hard cock. As the elevator opened, Jace jerked Sam by the belt loops out into the hall. "Come with me," he growled.

Before Sam knew what was happening, Jace had Sam inside his room. Their lips connected again in an all out assault of teeth and tongue, Sam giving back as good as he got. His zipper was opened and his jeans pushed down in moments.

Sam struggled to get his shoes and his jeans off without breaking their explosive kiss. Jace's hands found his ass and ran a finger up the crease. When he discovered the plug, he groaned.

Breaking the kiss, Jace spun Sam around and bent him over the bed. He could hear a zipper sliding down and then Jace's long thick cock was sliding across his ass. "Ready to be fucked?" Jace asked, moving the plug in and out.

Sam's back bowed with pleasure, presenting himself even more to Jace's gaze. "Yessss," he hissed. "Fuck me."

In one skilled move, Jace removed the plug and shoved his cock in to the hilt. "Uhhh," Sam groaned at the combination of pleasure and pain. "Do it," he said.

Gripping Sam's hips, Jace thrust his cock in and out of Sam's already stretched hole. "Fuck you feel good," Jace growled, picking up his pace.

Sam had never felt anything like it. The raw animalistic passion Jace exuded was more exciting than anything he'd experienced. "Harder," he panted.

As Jace pounded into him, he began talking. The more lost he became, the more spilled from his mouth.

"You've been teasing me with this ass of yours for too long," Jace growled.

Wrapping his hand around his throbbing cock, Sam spurted his seed onto the brown and blue bedspread. "Shit!" he yelled.

A few more thrusts and Jace buried himself as deep as he could inside Sam's ass and came. Sam felt the sticky cum running down his perineum to drip onto the spread along with his own.

Jace collapsed against Sam's back and struggled to regain his breath. As his cock softened, it slid from Sam's chute.

He was about to turn over and take Jace into his arms, when he felt the man in question go rigid. All too soon the warmth of Jace's body was gone and Sam could hear him mumbling to himself. Turning over, Sam sat on the edge of the bed.

"Next time you're hungry for a meaningless fuck, watch where you look for it." Jace gave Sam one last look before disappearing into the bathroom.

Unsure of what to do, Sam gathered his clothes. Meaningless? Is that what it had been to Jace? Sam zipped his jeans and walked out of the room, still holding his shoes in his hand.

* * * *

"Hi, Mom," Sam said into the phone as he took off his shoes.

"Hi, Sammy, how's school?"

"Fine. We're still on break. Actually, I'm in Miami for that new job I started. The owner wanted me to look at some more files to see if I need to scan them into Bianchi Bytes computer system."

"Woo, Miami. You're a regular corporate executive," she teased.

"Stop," he said as he unwrapped the sub sandwich he'd purchased down in the coffee shop.

"So what are you doing calling your mom when you should be out enjoying the city?"

"Just thought I'd stay in this evening. It was a long day in a hot storage building. I think I'll eat a little something and then grab a shower before turning in early."

"Is there something wrong? You don't sound like yourself."

"No, there's nothing wrong. Just hot and tired. I'll call you when I get back to school."

"Okay. Try to at least enjoy a little of your time there."

"I will. I promise."

Sam hung up his cell phone and tossed it on the nightstand. It had been one of the worst days of his life. He'd worked side by side with Jace and Phil all day. Hell, Jace wouldn't even look him in the eyes.

Jace may regret what happened between them, but that was no reason to treat Sam like a piece of shit. At least the trip would be over soon and he could get back to his friends.

After several bites of his sandwich, Sam wrapped it back up. It had been the same at lunch. Phil had gone out and brought them back Cuban sandwiches. Not wanting to hurt Phil's feelings, Sam made an excuse about wanting to walk the area while he ate. As soon as he was out of eyesight, he dumped the sandwich into the nearest garbage can.

Not wanting to smell onions in his room for the next day and a half, Sam went out to the hall to dump the uneaten sandwich and came face to face with Jace.

Turning around quickly, Sam headed back to his room.

"Wait, I need to talk to you," Jace called after him.

"Not interested in anything you have to say," Sam said scanning his key card before disappearing back into his room.

He still wasn't sure whether to be hurt or pissed over the whole situation. All he knew right then was he needed a shower, bad. He pulled off his dusty T-shirt and stuffed it into a plastic bag provided by the hotel.

Walking into the bathroom, Sam turned on the water and stripped out of the rest of his clothes before stepping under the spray. With the water pounding down on his face, he was suddenly glad he was alone. Crying was for wusses.

Chapter Four

"Hey, you're back early," Bear said, as Sam walked into BK.

"Yeah, we finished up, so I didn't see any reason to stay," Sam continued past Bear to the stairs. "I'll catch up with you later if that's okay?"

"Sure," Bear replied.

Sam gave a polite knock to the door before barging in. He doubted Lark was entertaining, but it was the right thing to do. "Hey," he waved to his roommate and set his bags down.

Lark was sitting on his bed with a text book on his lap. He adjusted his small wire-frame glasses and looked up at Sam. "I didn't think you'd be home until Sunday night."

Sam shrugged. "Change of plans. I hope you didn't have anything planned for the night. I can always crash on the couch downstairs."

Grinning, Lark held up his organic chemistry book. "Just refreshing my brain."

He took his shoes off and fell onto his bed. "You amaze me. Here it is, the last party night of spring break and you're studying."

Lark's mouth turned down as he looked out the window. "School work doesn't come naturally to me. I have to work a lot harder than most people."

"Maybe you should've chosen an easier major, then. Anything in the science field is gonna be tough."

"Maybe, but science is what I love, so it's worth it to me."

Sam studied Lark as he went back to his book. He'd never really looked at him before. Lark was one of those guys people tended to not see.

He was small, not just short or skinny but both. Sam doubted Lark was over five-three or four, with blond hair and glasses. Back home, they would've referred to Lark as a nerd. At college, Lark just seemed to be swallowed up by the mass of people always roaming around campus.

Sam undressed and wrapped his towel around his waist. "I'm gonna take a shower and then turn in."

"Okay," Lark said absently, never taking his eyes from his book.

Rolling his eyes, Sam grabbed his kit out of his duffle and headed to the bathroom. He set his stuff down on a bench and stepped into one of the stalls. Just as the water was heating up, Liam popped his head over the short wall.

"Have fun?"

"No," Sam answered and rinsed the shampoo from his hair. Sure he'd had fun for about twenty minutes, but the pain he'd endured at the hand of Jace's flip comment and attitude hadn't been worth it.

"Bummer," Liam said. "What happened? You didn't get along with Jace?"

Carol Lynne

"Something like that." He knew he probably shouldn't say anything, but he really needed someone to talk to. "He gave me a pity fuck. Although at the time it seemed like the real thing."

Liam's brows shot up. "Jace did that? You want me to have Bear whoop his ass?"

Sam laughed for the first time in what seemed like ages. "Naw. I learned my lesson."

"So what're you gonna do when you see him at work?"

"Not sure yet. I was thinking of quitting, but I really need the money. You're lucky. You get to do your work from here."

Sam finished washing and turned off the water. Giving himself a quick dry, he wrapped the towel around himself and got out. Picking up his kit, Sam walked towards the sink. It wasn't until he opened it that he remembered his plug. "Shit," he mumbled.

"What?" Liam asked, coming up behind him.

"Nothing, just left something in Miami." He pulled out his comb and started working on the mass of curls.

Liam leaned his hip against the sink and crossed his arms. "Bear and I are going to watch a movie with Charlie. You're more than welcome to join us."

Sam turned to Liam. He really was a good friend. Probably the best he'd ever had. "Thanks, but I'm gonna turn in early."

Liam placed a hand on Sam's shoulder. "Come find me if you need to talk. You know my door's always open."

"Yeah, I know." Liam straightened and started to leave. "Hey, Liam?" His friend looked over his shoulder. "Thanks," Sam said. Liam gave him a nod and walked out.

* * * *

Monday afternoon, Sam was busy going through a box of files when a knock sounded at the door. Thinking it was Tony, who said he'd be down to check on Sam's progress, he opened it right away.

As soon as Sam saw Jace's scowl, he tried to shut the door. "Go away."

Jace pushed the door open enough for him to come in, before shutting it again. "We need to talk."

"I told you before. I have nothing to say to you." Sam went back to his desk and turned his back on his visitor.

"Is that why you skipped out of Miami on me? Hell, I didn't even know you'd left until I waited in the lobby to leave for the airport. I had to call Tony to find out you'd taken off on Saturday."

Sam didn't say a word. He didn't owe Jace any explanations.

A sun bronzed hand appeared over his shoulder, setting something down in front of him. Even though the object was wrapped in a handkerchief, Sam knew it was his plug. He closed his eyes at the humiliation. Of all the things he could've left, why did it have to be something so personal? He imagined Jace had a pretty good laugh over it after he left.

Again, Sam said nothing.

"What? You're not talking to me?" Jace paced the small area behind Sam's chair.

"Isn't that what you want? Don't worry, I won't go chasing after you again. I learned my lesson."

Jace sighed heavily. "I forgot protection. I need to know if you're clean."

Sam rolled his eyes. Perfect. All this and no apology, only a demand that he give up his medical records. "Yeah. Are you?"

"Yes, but maybe you should've taken the time to find out before we fucked. This is exactly the reason I refuse to date a kid."

Sam felt his face go red, not from embarrassment but anger. He stood and spun around, getting right in Jace's face. "Me? I had fuckin' condoms in my pocket. You're the one that was so hot to get his dick in me he didn't think. So tell me, Mr. Macho Corporate Executive, who's the irresponsible one? Get the fuck out of my office. No, better yet, I'll leave." Sam grabbed his jacket and lunch sack and pushed passed Jace. He didn't stop walking until he reached the bus stop.

"Fuck that," he shouted.

* * * *

Tony met him in the hall when he returned from lunch. "My office, now," Tony said and turned away.

Jace rubbed the back of his neck and followed his boss. He knew this was coming. He should've known better than to confront Sam at work. He'd just been so pissed when he found out Sam had skipped out on him.

When he walked into Tony's office, his friend was leaning against the desk with his arms crossed. "Shut the door," he instructed.

After doing what he'd been told, Jace stood in front of Tony.

"What the hell happened in Miami?"

"We got the job done you sent us for," Jace said, crossing his own arms.

"That's not all you did apparently, or Sam wouldn't have quit."

Jace was shocked. He knew how much Sam needed the job from talking to Charlie. "He quit?"

"Spill it," Tony demanded.

Accepting defeat, Jace sat in one of the chairs. "I slept with him. Well, that's not really true. I fucked him."

"And?"

"And that was it." Tony was a friend and his boss, but he didn't plan on telling him what an ass he'd made out of himself. He certainly didn't plan on telling him that he'd been so out of his mind with lust he'd forgotten to use protection.

Tony studied him for a few moments. "You and I both know there's more to it, but I won't push. I suggest you work it out with Sam. Whatever it is, you ran him away and now you can bring him back."

"I can't," Jace growled. "He's too much temptation for me, and right now I need to have my head on straight. I've got too much on my plate as it is. I don't have time to be thinking of a twenty-one year old with the prettiest grey eyes I've ever seen."

Tony walked over and put his hand on Jace's shoulder. "You can't let what's happening with Kade ruin your life."

Jace let out a sarcastic chuckle. "Tell that to him. He's moving in on Wednesday."

"Oh, Jace," Tony sighed and shook his head. "Are you sure that's the right thing to do?"

No. He wasn't sure about anything anymore except he loved Kade and would do anything for him. "He needs me."

"And when do you take care of your needs? Sam may be young, but he's a good man. If you like him, don't fuck it up with some moral sense of obligation to Kade."

* * * *

"What're you doing here?" Bear asked Jace as he walked into the kitchen.

"I'm looking for Sam," he said.

Jace was a fairly big guy, but when Bear walked over and towered above him, Jace had to rethink his position.

Bear leaned down, face inches from Jace's. "Gimmee one reason I shouldn't kick your butt right out that front door."

"I'm here to apologise," Jace answered, hoping it was enough to pacify the giant.

It must have been because Bear took a step back. "He's in the computer room." Bear narrowed his eyes. "Upset him more than he is and prepare to die."

Normally Jace would take the words as a bluff, but looking at the angry face in front of him, he wasn't so sure. Instead of giving Bear an answer he gave a nod and left.

How had he let things get to this point? What the hell was wrong with him lately? Yeah, he had a mess of personal stuff going on, but he'd never in his life been intentionally cruel to a person. Especially not someone he thought about night and day. Maybe it was self-defence?

If he didn't admit to his feelings and definite attraction to Sam, he wouldn't feel as lousy when Sam found someone else…and he would. Jace had no doubts about that. Sam was young and still testing his wings. He was surrounded on a daily basis by gorgeous gay men, who could ever expect Sam to be faithful?

Arriving at the computer room, Jace looked through the window. Sam and Liam were working side by side. Jace hesitated. Would Liam get in his face like his mountainous lover?

Deciding it didn't matter, Jace opened the door and stuck his head in. "Sam? Can I have a word with you?"

Both men stopped typing and turned to face him. Liam looked at Jace with disgust in his eyes. *Yeah*, Jace thought, *I know the feeling.*

Liam turned to Sam. "You want me to leave?"

Sam looked at Jace before turning back to his computer. "It's okay. He can't hurt me anymore."

Liam rose and walked towards the door. Before going out he looked up at Jace. "Fix this," he whispered.

Jace nodded.

After Liam left, Jace took his seat. "I came to apologise."

"Okay, so say you're sorry and get out." Sam continued to type, barely acknowledging Jace's presence.

"Can you at least look at me?" Jace wanted nothing more than to pull Sam into his arms and kiss those shadows from beneath his eyes.

Sam's fingers hesitated over the keyboard for several seconds. "Why?" Sam bowed his head. "I thought I'd been hurt in the past, but what you've done to me is beyond hurt. I don't know that I can look at you and not break down. I know that makes me less in your eyes, but it's the truth."

Jace couldn't take it any more. He reached out and placed a hand on Sam's down turned head. "I brought you something." He dug the sheet of paper out of his coat pocket and set it on the keyboard.

With shaking hands, Sam unfolded the results of Jace's blood tests. Sam looked at the paper then handed it back to him. "I've got one just like it upstairs."

"I just wanted you to know that I was clean." Jace took the paper and stuffed it back in his pocket. "I'm sorry I hurt you." He leaned over and kissed Sam's temple. "I acted like an ass. I know that. I knew it when I was doing it, but I was trying to push you away."

"Well it worked," Sam mumbled.

"I don't have time for a boyfriend, and you don't deserve anything less than someone's full attention."

Sam finally looked at him. "Was that so hard to say? I can tell you it would've hurt a hell of a lot less than the way you chose to push me away."

"I'm sorry," he said, cupping Sam's jaw. "If things were different I'd take you to my bed and never let you leave."

Sam leaned into Jace's touch for a moment before pulling away. "Okay. You've said what you need to, you can leave."

Jace felt like he'd been dismissed. "Come back to work," he said.

Sam's spine stiffened. "Is that what all this was about? What, Tony tell you to do whatever it took to get me back?"

"No, well, yes, but that's not why I said the things I did."

Sam licked his lips and chuckled. "Tell Tony I'll be there." He turned back to his computer and started typing again. "You can go, your job is done."

Jace's hands hovered in mid-air. *Just reach out to him*, he told himself. A vision of Kade sprang to mind and Jace pulled back. "I'll see you around, Sam."

"Not if I see you first," Sam commented.

Chapter Five

"Come on, we're getting you out of this funk one way or another," Liam said, poking Sam in the side. "I know you got paid, so you can't use the old excuse of you can't afford it."

Sam swatted Liam's hand away. "Promise me if I do this, we won't stay long."

"Okay, but Nate wants a beer. Since he's been off the football team, he thinks he needs at least one drink every Friday." Liam grinned. "I indulge him because he's even friskier when he has alcohol in his system."

Laughing, Sam sat up. "Am I okay like this, or do I need to change?"

Liam took in his ripped jeans and tight red T-shirt. "You look good to me, but don't you dare tell Nate I said that."

Sam held up his hands in surrender. "Do I look like a man with a suicide wish? No way am I gonna tell Bear his boyfriend was checking out my goods."

Liam punched him in the arm. "I was not checking out your goods, just your clothes, and the way they're moulded to every inch of your body," Liam said with a wink.

Wrapping his arm around his friend's neck, Sam led them to the kitchen to find Bear.

"You ready?" Liam asked.

Bear growled and removed Sam's arm before replacing it with his own. "I am now."

Taking the bus, they arrived at McGilley's Pub just in time for the end of happy hour. "Quick, let's order a bunch of appetizers. They're half-price for the next ten minutes," Bear said.

"Spoken like a true college student," Sam chuckled.

They got the waitress's attention and placed their order with five minutes to spare. Liam was busy teasing Bear about the amount of food he could consume and Sam started looking around.

He froze when his gaze landed on Jace. "That sonofabitch," he ground out. Jace was sitting at a small table with another man. Not just any man, but one of the baddest looking biker-types he'd ever seen.

As he watched them, Jace started laughing. His whole face changed when he laughed. Gorgeous all the time, the happy expression made Jace devastating.

Sam felt his hands shake. He didn't know if it was anger or hurt. Without thinking he stood.

"Sam? What's wrong?" Bear asked.

"I gotta take care of something," he said, before heading over to the laughing couple.

He walked up and put his hands on his hips. "Is he why you didn't have time for me? You know, if you wanted to fuck the field, you could've just told me. You're pathetic," he added before turning around and walking back to his table.

Liam and Bear were looking right at him as he approached. "Sorry, guys, I don't feel much like dinner. I'll catch you back at the house."

Sam left, but instead of heading back to the dorm, he went to the park. He needed to clear his head in private.

* * * *

Watching Sam walk away broke Jace's heart.

"Who was that?" Kade asked.

"Sam," Jace replied.

"You two have somethin' going?"

Jace looked at his friend and former roommate. "No. Not really."

"But you'd like to," Kade surmised.

Shrugging, Jace looked down at his half-eaten dinner. Did he? Yeah. Unfortunately life was complicated.

"It would never work," he finally said.

"In other words, you don't feel like putting the effort into a relationship with him."

"No, that's not what I mean," Jace defended himself. "Sam's sensitive, hot, young, damn is he young."

Kade covered Jace's hand. "You're scared he'll do what I did. Have you been carrying this around for twelve years?"

"I don't know, maybe," Jace turned his hand over and threaded his fingers through Kade's.

"Not everyone's a cheater. I was young and stupid. It was the first time away from home and I thought I had to sample everything out there." Kade leaned forward across the table. "Now look at me. I'm paying for my sins. You don't need to do that for me."

Jace thought about what his friend had said. He could see Kade's point. Jace had been paying for Kade's infidelity. He hadn't allowed himself to get close with a lover since. One night stands were fine when all you needed was release, but they did little for the soul.

"Doesn't matter now. I've already lost any chance I once had with Sam."

Kade released his hand and sat back, his muscles testing the seams of his leather jacket. "I don't know what went on between the two of you, but if you give up on someone you really want, you're a fool."

"That's me, Jace-The-Fool-Rawlings." He wiped his mouth and threw his napkin over the remains of his dinner. "You ready to get out of here?"

"Sure," Kade said.

Once in the car, Kade turned to him. "Where does Sam live?"

"Why?"

"Just wondered," Kade replied looking out the side window.

"BK House, remember I drove you by it Wednesday when you got in."

"Oh, yeah, the dorm."

"Yeah." Jace tapped his fingers on the steering wheel.

Kade reached out and put a hand on his arm. "Why don't you drop by the house and talk to him?"

He wanted to, god how he wanted to. "What could I say that would make a difference?"

"The truth."

Jace shook his head. "I'd never do that to you."

"Hell, Jace, I'd be homeless if it weren't for you. I'm not about to come between you and this guy. Tell him. I'm a big boy. I can take care of myself."

"You sure you don't mind?"

"Nope. Go on by. I'll wait in the car."

"That's bullshit. You can at least come in and meet Charlie."

Kade nodded. "I've heard a lot about that guy over the last several weeks. I'd like to meet him."

With that settled, Jace turned the car around and drove towards BK. He wasn't exactly sure what he was going to say, but if Sam would listen, he'd get down on his knees to beg for forgiveness.

* * * *

Crossing the parking lot, Sam spotted Jace's car. "Shit." He looked at his watch. It was almost ten. He knew if Jace hadn't left by now, he wouldn't go until Sam got home.

Steeling himself for a battle, he opened the front door. The sight that met him stopped him in his tracks. Charlie, that biker dude and Lark, were sitting in the living room laughing up a storm.

Sam didn't know Lark knew how to laugh. "What's going on?"

Kade stood, and wiped his hands on his jeans. "Hi, um…I'm Kade."

Sam nodded, but said nothing.

"Jace is up in your room. I hope you don't mind, but it's kinda important that he talks to you."

"I've got nothing to say to Jace." Sam walked into the kitchen with Kade close on his heels.

"Hold up," Kade said. "Just give me a second."

Sam looked at the man in front of him. Six-four at least with shoulder length black hair, goatee, and tattoos, a whole boat load of tattoos. "Look, I didn't mean to step on your toes. You want Jace, you got him."

Kade grinned. "You're a feisty little thing. And whether I want Jace or not isn't the issue." Kade pushed his hair out of his face to reveal sparkling blue eyes. "I'm not gonna stand here and tell you I don't have feelings for him, but what we had was over a long time ago. He loved me, and I fucked it up by not being able to keep my dick in my pants. It didn't matter that I had someone as wonderful as that man upstairs. I wanted more, always more."

Sam walked to the fridge and got out two bottles of Charlie's beer and handed one to Kade. "So why are you here?"

"Wow, you cut right to the chase, don't you?" Kade joked. "I got sick a couple of months ago and lost my job and apartment. I'd already lost my family several years ago when I told them I was HIV positive. Jace was the only one I could think of who'd be willing to help me out until I could get back on my feet."

HIV positive? The man in front of him looked healthy as a horse. "Seriously?"

"Yeah. Jace's been helping me through it. I get depressed sometimes and call him in the middle of the night. I can't tell you how many times he's stayed up just talking to me."

Kade put a hand on Sam's shoulder. "He's a good guy and he really likes you, but I think I burned him pretty badly. Trust doesn't come easy with him, and when he looks at you, he sees a young, sexy college guy."

What Kade was trying to say finally dawned on him. "And he's afraid I'm going to do to him what you did."

"Bingo."

"I wouldn't, you know?"

Kade looked at him for several moments. "Yeah, I think I know. He's upstairs trying to figure out how to apologise to you."

"Well then maybe I shouldn't keep him waiting. Are you okay down here for a while longer?"

"Sure. Lark and I were just talking about watching the Saturday night horror movie." Kade looked up at the kitchen clock. "It'll be on in ten minutes. By my calculations, that'll give the two of you at least two hours to make up."

Sam grinned. "How can someone who looks so tough have a heart as big as yours?"

Kade laughed. "Contracting HIV is a very humbling experience. It tends to change a person from the inside out."

Sam reached out and shook Kade's hand. "Thanks. And tell Lark thanks. Actually, I think if I'm not mistaken, I saw Lark laugh earlier. That was a first."

Kade's brows drew together. "What do you mean? He seems like a nice guy."

"Oh he's very nice, just kind of sombre and bookish." Sam finished his beer and threw it in the recycling tub. "Don't tell Charlie we drank his beer. I'll buy him some more before he realises it's missing."

* * * *

Sam stood outside his door for several minutes before he had the courage to venture inside. After everything Kade had told him, Sam knew Jace was under pressure, but could that cancel out all the things he'd said?

Turning the knob, he went in. Jace was sitting on the end of Sam's bed with his head in his hands. As soon as he heard the door close, he sprang up and faced Sam.

"I heard you want to talk to me," Sam said, coming further into the room to take a seat at his desk.

"Yes," Jace answered. "I wanted to apologise. I know I've acted like a complete ass, and I have absolutely no right to even be here, but I needed to see you."

Sam could see the distress in Jace's brown eyes. "Okay, talk." He may be willing to listen, but he wasn't going to just lie down and forgive him on the spot.

Jace rubbed his hands together and sat on the bed facing Sam. "Years ago I was hurt deeply by someone I thought I could trust…"

"Kade," Sam interrupted to insert the name.

Jace looked surprised. "Yes. How did you know?"

"I talked to him downstairs. He seems like a good guy."

"Now. He wasn't always."

"I gathered that. Go on." Sam crossed his arms and watched Jace squirm. He knew it was cruel, because he also knew he'd forgive him, eventually, but Jace deserved to squirm a bit first.

As Jace went on to tell Sam about Kade's infidelity and their subsequent break-up, he simply nodded.

"I can't lie to you anymore. When I first started hanging around BK it was out of loneliness. I was new in town and wanted to get to know people. I didn't count on my strong attraction to you. When you asked me out that day, I freaked. I saw the past repeating itself and lashed out."

"Okay, that explains the reason you were a jerk then, but what about Miami?"

Jace had the decency to look down at the floor. "I tried to stay away, but when I saw that jerk's hands on you…I snapped. I took you like an animal and to top it off, I didn't use protection. I'm living with someone with HIV and I didn't even think about protecting you."

"So most of that other stuff you said about not having time was just bullshit," Sam surmised.

Jace looked up and leaned forward, staring Sam in the eyes. "Yes and no. I want you, god I can't begin to explain how much, but between work and Kade..."

"Kade seems like the kind of guy who can take care of himself. As far as your job? I have school and work. It would be nice to know I have something to look forward to at the end of the day."

Nodding, Jace reached out and put his hand on Sam's knee. "Kade's in an upswing at the present time, but it could change any moment. He's been severely depressed. I keep telling him his life isn't over just because he's been diagnosed, but he doesn't believe it."

Sam thought about the man he'd met downstairs. He wondered if he'd get jealous if Jace spent too much time with him. Yeah, probably, but what was his other option? To walk away from the one man he wanted?

"I can try to deal with your relationship with Kade," Sam mumbled.

Jace fell in front of Sam on his knees. "You will? Does that mean you'll give me another chance?"

"Yeah, but I'm not going to just fall into your arms this time. I don't think you realise how much you've hurt me. I'd be willing to start slow though. Go out, get to know each other, and then we can see where it leads."

Jace started to embrace him, but stopped himself. "Is it okay if I hold you? Nothing more, I just need to feel you in my arms."

Sam stood and pulled Jace up. He wrapped his arms around the bigger man and laid his head on Jace's chest. "One day at a time."

Chapter Six

Two weeks later, Sam was putting away a finished file box when he heard the door open. He grinned to himself. The only one who knew the security combination that would just walk in without knocking was Jace.

"Is it quitting time already?" he asked.

Strong arms wrapped around his waist as a soft set of lips landed on his neck. "Mmm," Jace moaned. "Not quite, but I'm having a bad day. So I decided to take a break."

Sam spun in his arms and kissed him, thrusting his tongue deep. He felt the evidence of Jace's desire rub against him and groaned. "We need to stop."

"Don't wanna stop," Jace said pulling Sam's shirt out of his pants.

They'd been on numerous dates since they'd made up, but this was the first time Jace had allowed his control to slip. Sam was flattered, but he couldn't risk losing his job. Jace's fingers explored Sam's chest, stopping to pinch and play with his pebbled nipples.

"Jace," Sam said, leaning into Jace's touch. "Really, we can't do this."

"I need you," Jace replied, falling to his knees.

"Not here." Damn he wished he weren't so loyal to the company. The pressure of Jace's face against his steel hard erection, almost wore him down. "Tonight," he moaned as Jace nipped at his cock through his pants. "I'll come over to your place."

That seemed to splash some cold water on Jace. He released his hold on Sam and stood. "I don't know if that'll work. Kade's been depressed again lately."

Sam shook his head. "Well we can't be alone at BK. Lark never leaves the room."

Jace nuzzled Sam's neck and jaw. "Hotel. I'll get a room."

Memories of their Miami romp came to mind. "No, too impersonal. Talk to Kade. I'm sure he'd give us an evening alone if you asked."

Jace's thigh pressed against Sam's throbbing erection. His resolve almost crumbled as goose bumps broke out over his arms and stomach. "Please talk to Kade. I need you, too." He reached down and ran his hand over Jace's cock.

"I'll call him," Jace growled. "If he won't go out, I'll make him put on headphones. I plan to make you scream."

Sam had no doubt Jace would keep his word on that. He was at the soft whimpers stage now and they were both fully dressed. He looked at the clock over Jace's shoulder. "Another hour and I'm all yours."

Jace grabbed Sam's ass and ground himself against him. "You're already mine. I just need time to prove it to you."

* * * *

Barely an hour later, Jace was back, tapping his watch. "Come on, let's get out of here."

He watched as Sam nodded and shrugged into his jacket. "Should we leave separately? I don't want to give anyone the idea that I'm getting special treatment because I'm sleeping with the boss."

Jace chuckled. "Well if you consider getting an office in a storage room to be a perk, then you haven't been in the corporate world long enough." He wrapped his arms around Sam and gave him a short but deep kiss. "Besides, the people around here need to get used to you and I being together."

Sam's face brightened, a soft grin playing around those sexy lips Jace loved to kiss. "Okay."

Turning off the lights, Jace hurried Sam out of the room. He sent up a wave to Nancy as they passed by the reception desk. As soon as they were out the front door, he took Sam's hand. "Do you want to get something for dinner on the way to my place?"

Sam seemed to think about it for a moment. "Will Kade be there?"

Jace unlocked his new Jaguar and opened Sam's door. "Yeah, I'm sorry. He said he had a movie to watch though and would try to stay in his room and not bother us."

"In that case, I think we should call him and see if he wants something to eat. It'd be polite if we at least ate dinner with him."

Sam climbed in and Jace went around and got behind the wheel. "You're a great guy," he said. Leaning over the console, he put a hand to the back of Sam's neck and pulled him in for a kiss.

Opening for him immediately, Sam's tongue tangled with his. Jace could feel his raging need return. He knew he needed to slow down. He'd promised himself this time he'd take the time to show Sam exactly how much he meant to him.

Pulling back, he looked into Sam's deep grey eyes. "I'll call him." He opened his phone and pressed the speed dial.

"Hello," Kade's deep voice answered.

"Hey, we're heading out and wondered what you felt like eating for dinner?"

"I don't care. You know I'm pretty easy when it comes to food."

"Yes, I know, and I'm getting you something with vegetables."

"Ahh, Mom," Kade teased.

"If I didn't look after your diet, who would? Certainly not you." Jace looked over and winked at Sam.

"Whatever. Just make sure there's some meat
to go along with all the veggies."

"Yes, sir," Jace said and disconnected.

Sam put a hand on Jace's thigh. "You're a good friend to him. Does he get sick often?"

"No. Other than the HIV he's as healthy as a horse physically."

Sam had a confused look on his face. "But Kade told me he'd lost his job and home because he'd been sick."

Starting the car, Jace wondered how much he could say without invading Kade's right to privacy. "For Kade, the only illness he battles is mental."

Jace was surprised when Sam didn't ask him to go into details. "I think we should go by the grocery store. I'll make the vegetables while you grill us some steaks. We'll put Kade in charge of dessert."

Reaching across the console, Jace ran his hand over the bulge in Sam's pants. "I don't need any dessert besides you."

Sam grinned. "Good answer."

* * * *

"It was great of you to do this," Kade said as he cleared the table, something he had insisted upon.

"It was nice," Sam replied. "We should do it more often."

"Maybe we should have a barbeque when it gets a little warmer outside." Jace pulled Sam out of his chair and onto his lap.

"Have you ever been to one of Luc and Justin's backyard parties? I went to one in the fall. Maybe something like that would be fun. All three of us need to meet people."

Jace's brows shot up. "Hopefully you're talking about gaining new friends and not lovers."

Sam curled against his man. "You're the only lover I need."

"Speaking of which," Kade interrupted, "why don't the two of you call it a night? I'll finish up these dishes and retire to my room for the evening."

Without another word, Jace stood with Sam still in his arms and carried him down the hall to the master suite. Setting Sam on his feet, Jace began to unbutton his own shirt.

Sam licked his lips as Jace's perfect swimmer's body was revealed. "Gorgeous," he whispered as he pulled his shirt over his head.

Seconds later, they were both undressed and hard. Sam was thankful they'd gotten their tests out of the way, as he gazed upon Jace's ruddy cock. He spotted a pearly drop of pre-cum glistening at the top of Jace's perfectly shaped crown. Without thought, Sam bent and licked the head of Jace's cock.

The taste was overwhelming. Sam fell to his knees, hungry for more. He ran his tongue up the heavily veined shaft and closed his mouth over the top, taking as much of the thick length into his mouth as he could.

Jace moaned and buried his fingers in Sam's curls. "Good," Jace groaned and started shallow thrusts in and out of Sam's mouth.

Sam moaned around Jace's cock as he took hold of his own and began to stroke. He knew this was only round one. They would both get it up again, so he didn't worry when he felt his approaching orgasm.

"Gonna," Jace panted.

Sam backed off enough to swirl his tongue around the plump crown. He didn't intend to miss a single drop of Jace's seed.

The first stream hit the back of his throat, so Sam backed off even more as he shot his own cum into his hand.

Jace's fingers gripped Sam's hair in a tight fist as he continued to come. "Good, oh god, so good."

Before Sam released his hold, he dipped his tongue into Jace's slit and retrieved the last drop. Jace pulled Sam up and devoured his mouth. Sam shared the flavour of Jace's essence still clinging to his tongue..

Breaking apart, Jace looked at Sam. "You're gonna kill me, aren't you?"

Sam smiled. "I'm sure as hell gonna try."

Chapter Seven

A hard cock nudging his hole woke Sam the following morning. "Hmmm, morning."

"Morning, baby. Are you sore?"

"Not that sore." Sam nuzzled his ass against Jace's length.

Pushing in slowly, Jace groaned. "I love the feel of you around my cock."

Sam chuckled. "Yeah, I'm pretty fond of having you inside me, as well." He remembered their exploratory loving the previous night. They'd spent hours touching and kissing as well as having mind blowing sex.

As Jace moved in and out of his body, Sam felt warm and loved. He knew it was way too early in their relationship to bring that word into play, but this is where he was meant to be. Sam felt it in his soul.

Jace buried his face in Sam's hair. He nuzzled around a few moments before warm lips landed on the back of Sam's neck. "I want to mark you," Jace whispered, seconds before his mouth was firmly attached to Sam's skin.

The harder Jace sucked, the faster his hips moved.

Sam wrapped his hand around his cock. "Feel's so good."

A grunt from Jace was his only answer.

Jace wrapped his hand around Sam's and pressed his thumb against the slit in the crown.

Sam groaned as his cock erupted, shooting warmth over both their hands.

Jace released his hold on Sam's neck and buried his length as deep as he could before filling him with his hot seed. Sam barely caught the words 'I love you' before they slipped from his lips.

The way Jace held him was almost reverent. "I like waking up with you," Sam said.

"Mmm hmm. I'd love to make it a regular occurrence." Jace withdrew and helped Sam turn in his arms. "How does that sound to you?"

"Perfect." Sam pressed his lips to Jace's and thrust his tongue inside, sweeping the interior of his lover's mouth. The alarm began beeping and Jace reached over his shoulder to shut it off.

Groaning, Sam ran his tongue over Jace's heavy morning beard. "I need to get back to the dorm and get changed for class."

A warm hand landed on Sam's ass. "What time will classes end?"

Grinding himself against Jace, Sam tried to think. "Um, it's my short day. The last one is over at eleven."

"I'll pick you up in front of BK and take you to lunch before work. Does that sound agreeable?"

Sam grinned, feeling a little giddy. "Only if we can get something to go and find some place to neck for the rest of the lunch hour."

"You read my mind." Jace rimmed Sam's hole with his finger.

* * * *

A week later, Sam was bummed. He'd received his first C on a test. He knew he should spend less time fucking and more time studying, but the last few weeks had been the best of his life.

"Why the long face, Mr. Howard?"

Sam turned to find Jack standing at the stove, preparing dinner for the guys in the house.

"Got a sucky grade on a test."

Jack turned from the stove and crossed his arms. "You know what to do about it, don't you? Perhaps spending a little more time doing what your parents are paying for would help."

"Parent, singular," Sam corrected.

"Oh, sorry. I thought Charlie said you were Aaron's brother."

"Half-brother. His dad messed around on his wife and got my mom pregnant. He was too ashamed of himself to come around when I was growing up."

Jack's facial expression froze for several seconds. Sam was about to apologise for anything he might have said to upset him, when Jack spoke. "Sometimes we do what we think is the best thing only to find out we were wrong. It's not easy to undo a mistake made when we were young. Could be your dad regrets the decision he made, but is afraid to do anything about it?"

Sam nodded. He had a feeling Jack was speaking from personal experience, but he wasn't the type of man to let people in. "Maybe," Sam mumbled.

"Dinner will be ready at eighteen-hundred hours."

"Thanks, Jack." Sam swung his backpack over his shoulder and walked to his room.

He wasn't at all surprised to see Lark sitting on the bed studying. "That's what I should be doing." He threw his pack on the bed and flopped down.

"Problem?" Lark asked, pushing up his glasses.

Sam had never talked to his roommate about personal stuff, but Lark genuinely looked interested. "Kinda. I got a lower grade than normal on a test. It's my own damn fault. I've been spending all my time with Jace and haven't applied myself the way I used to. My problem is, I feel like I'm really enjoying life for the first time and don't want to lose that to studying."

Lark looked at Sam for a few brief moments before giving his head a small shake. "Sorry, but I'm not going to be much help to you. My existence is narrowed to this room and my classrooms. Okay, maybe I do stop in at the library occasionally." Lark grinned.

"I'm not sure what it would be like to have a life outside of class and studying." Lark gazed out the window the grin still present. "I think it would be worth the trade of a few bad grades."

"So why do you do it, study all the time?" Sam asked.

"What else do I have? I don't fit in, never have." Sam would swear he heard a catch in Lark's voice.

Damn. He realised at that moment he hadn't been a very good roommate. "Would you be interested in going to Jace's Friday? We're having a few couples over as part of our 'Get to know people' campaign."

Lark's teeth bit his bottom lip. Sam had seen the same habit many times when Lark was studying.

"I'd like to, but I've never really been to a dinner party. What do people talk about?"

"I don't know," Sam replied. "But you'll know me and you kind of know Jace. Kade will be there as well."

Lark nodded. "Yeah, they seem like nice people."

"They are. Come on, it'll be fun."

"Okay." Sam couldn't help notice the blush on Lark's face when he said it. Hmmm…

* * * *

"So how's the student teaching going?" Demitri asked.

"Good, real good. In fact, I have an interview next week with a junior high over in Longston."

"That would be handy. It would only take you what, twenty minutes to get there?"

"Yeah, of course I'd have to get a car first." Bear laughed.

Sam was snuggled against Jace's side listening to the different conversations in the room. With everyone's belly full, they were just lounging around talking.

Jace had been so cute earlier before their guests had arrived. Sam thought it was probably the first time he'd ever seen his man nervous. They'd only invited a few couples over besides Kade and Lark. Liam and Bear were there, of course, as well as Demitri and Aaron and Tony and Daniel. They'd invited Joe and Rocco, but unfortunately Rocco had come down with something at the last moment.

Sam grinned when he recalled Jace's blush when Aaron had commented on the choice of pies they had for dessert. Jace had coughed into his hand and admitted that a friend of his owned a bakery in Wyoming and he'd had Kyle ship them overnight to him.

Everyone at the table had insisted on getting Kyle's number before they left.

Sam listened to Demitri's smooth voice as he talked to Bear. Aaron seemed to hang on every word out of his lover's mouth. He couldn't help but watch his brother. He wanted to see a resemblance, but there simply wasn't one.

Feeling a set of lips kiss the top of his head, Sam looked up into Jace's brown eyes and smiled. "It's going good, yeah?"

"Real good," Jace answered and gave him a soft kiss on the lips.

Snuggling back in, Sam's eyes wandered to the only two single people in the room. Lark and Kade were both sitting on the floor, both looking a little uncomfortable. "Hey, Kade," Sam said. "Did I tell you Lark's never seen a Lethal Weapon movie?"

Kade turned to Lark. "You gotta be shittin' me?"

Lark's face turned an adorable shade of scarlet. "We didn't have televisions where I grew up. Every time Sam mentions the movie I don't know what he's talking about."

Sam noticed the looks that passed between the various couples in the room. No one knew Lark well enough to question him as to why he hadn't grown up with a TV.

Kade stood and held his hand out. "I can fix that. You have a couple of hours to kill? I've got all of them on DVD. We can go to the media room and I'll educate you on Mel Gibson."

Lark looked from Kade over to Sam. "What time did you want to leave?"

"Not for a while. Go on."

Lark took Kade's hand and stood. "Just let me know when you're ready," Lark said as he let Kade lead him from the room.

Jace gave Sam a squeeze. "You're not matchmaking are you? Because Kade won't get involved with anyone, and I don't want to see Lark get hurt."

Sam shrugged. "They both looked uncomfortable and bored. I was trying to help." He couldn't help but feel like he'd been scolded.

"Hey." Jace tapped Sam's nose.

When he looked at Jace, his lover kissed him. "I didn't mean that the way it sounded."

"Okay."

"Sam." Demitri's voice broke the tension between Sam and Jace.

"Yeah?"

"I was just wondering if Charlie and Jack were still going at it."

Sam chuckled and nodded his head. "Only when they're in the same room. I've never met two more stubborn men in my life."

Demitri laughed. "That's right. You haven't met my brother Alec yet."

"I don't see how he could possibly be worse than Charlie or Jack." Sam gave an exaggerated all over body shiver. "They scare me."

"I have a feeling they'll figure it out eventually. One of them just has to come off his high horse first. Then step back because BK might just go up in flames," Demitri said with a chuckle.

* * * *

By the time the last of their guests walked out the door, Jace was in need of a few serious kisses. It was hell sitting with Sam in his arms and not being able to touch or taste to his heart's content.

He pulled Sam against him and dove in. He swept his tongue through the interior of Sam's mouth, tasting the wine they'd sipped all evening.

Sam moaned and began rubbing against him. "I wish I could stay, but I promised Lark I'd ride home on the bus with him."

Jace reached down and unzipped Sam's jeans. Running his hand up the hard length of Sam's cock, he groaned. "I can ask Kade to take him home. I need you. You've been doing far too much studying lately. I miss my boyfriend."

Sam thrust against Jace's hand. "I miss you, too. Go ask Kade and then prepare yourself for the blowjob of a lifetime."

Chapter Eight

"Hey, baby." Jace's deep voice invaded his soul.

Sam smiled. "Hi. I was just thinking about you." Man he missed Jace like crazy. He'd only been in London for three days, and already Sam didn't know what to do with himself.

"Good thoughts, I hope?"

"Always," Sam replied. "So tell me how you're enjoying life in the big city."

"It's okay, but I'd be enjoying it a hell of a lot more if a certain grey-eyed man were with me."

"I am, in spirit anyway." Sam found a bench in the sunshine and sat down. He tilted his head back to feel the heat of the warm spring day on his face. "It's nice here for a change. I think winter has officially moved on."

"Not fair. It's raining in London."

"Sorry." Sam smiled. He wasn't really but it sounded convincing.

"I was wondering if you'd do me a favour? I've tried calling home for two days and I can't reach Kade. Would you mind going over to check on him? Maybe take him out for dinner or something?"

"You mean I get to finally drive the Jag?"

"Of course. Why haven't you been driving it? That's why I left it with you."

"I know, but I didn't see any reason to get attached. You'll be gone for two weeks. In that amount of time I could forget the bus schedule and then I'd be screwed," he joked.

"Drive the damn car. Forget the bus schedule, just don't forget about me."

"Never. I'll go by your place before I head to work."

"Thanks."

"Call me before you go to bed later. I might even be persuaded to talk dirty to you."

Jace groaned. "With an offer like that, I may have to turn in early."

"Not too early. I'm not about to have phone sex with you while sitting in a restaurant."

Sam heard Jace's soft growl. "Point taken. You'd better be alone when I make you come."

He wanted to tell Jace he loved him before he hung up, but he knew the first time should be face to face. "Miss you."

"Me, too. Call you later, and thanks for checking on Kade for me."

"No problem." Sam hung up and walked back to BK.

* * * *

Sam pounded on the door for what felt like twenty minutes. Giving up, he used the key Jace had given him. He knew Kade was there by the smoke-grey Harley parked in the driveway. He smiled to himself. He still remembered the argument Jace and Kade had gotten into about that bike. Jace tried to reason with Kade that it wasn't practical in Idaho not to have a car for winter. Kade had fired back that he didn't plan to stay that long.

"Kade," Sam hollered as he stepped inside. All the blinds had been pulled and not a light was on. "Hey, Kade, it's Sam. Are you busy?"

He spotted a big shadow moving down the hall. "What do you need, Sam?"

Sam turned to flip on the entry light, giving him enough illumination to at least see Kade's face. The dark circles under the bigger man's eyes and at least two days of growth on his face, attested to the fact that he was sliding back into a well of depression.

"I thought you might feel like going out to dinner later."

"No thanks. Tell Jace I don't need a babysitter." Kade turned and started to walk back towards his bedroom.

"Wait. You can't say something like that and just walk away." Sam went further into the room to follow Kade.

Kade spun and towered over him. "You got that wrong, Little Sammy. I can say damn near anything I want. It's what I can and can't do that's the problem. Now get out of here and leave me in peace."

From somewhere deep inside of himself, Sam's courage rose. Kade was a hell of a tough looking guy, but he was acting more like a child. "That attitude may work with Jace, but it doesn't pull any weight with me. Who knows, maybe it's because Jace loves you, but he gives into your emotions far too often."

"You don't know what the hell you're talking about, kid. Run along back to college. Jace is out of town, maybe you can get that roommate of yours to give it up…"

That was as far as Kade got before Sam slapped him across the face. Kade reacted on instinct and reared back and punched Sam in the nose.

His head flew back as he heard the loud crunch. Fuck! That hurt. Sam covered his nose and ran to the bathroom for a washcloth. When he glanced in the mirror, he saw that his nose was definitely not where it was supposed to be. He only hoped his insurance would cover everything.

Walking back into the hall, he was surprised to see Kade on the floor with his face in his hands. By the shaking shoulders, Sam could tell he was crying. "No time for that. I need you to drive me to the emergency room," Sam said. No way would he leave Kade here alone in this condition.

Kade looked up at him. "Huh? I fuckin' broke your nose and you want me to drive you?"

"Yeah. I think you owe it to me. Go get some clean clothes on and let's go." Kade looked at him for several seconds before disappearing into his bedroom.

While Kade changed, Sam rinsed the washcloth and called Lark.

"Hello?"

"Hey. Is there any way you can meet me at the hospital? Kade and I got into it and he busted my nose."

"Oh my god."

"Yeah, well, the real problem is Kade. He's depressed and I don't think he needs to be alone right now. Can you catch the bus and sit with him while they fix me up?"

"Sure. I'll leave now. It'll take me longer to

get there, but I'll make it."

"Thanks, Lark."

"Don't mention it."

Rinsing the cloth once more he went and stood by the door. "Any day, Kade," he yelled at the closed door.

"Coming." Kade was tucking in a sleeveless red T-shirt into a pair of holey jeans. He grabbed his black leather jacket off the back of the sofa and didn't stop until he was straddling his motorcycle.

"Um, I think it'd be better to take the car," Sam said and pointed towards his nose.

Kade started the bike. "I don't drive cars. If you want me to take you, hop on."

"Fine," Sam said. He climbed on the back of the bike and held on around Kade's waist with one hand while holding the cloth to his nose with the other.

As Kade roared out of the drive, all Sam could think about was Jace. What would he tell him? No way could he tell him the truth. The really stupid part was Sam totally blamed himself. He knew Kade was on edge as soon as he saw him. He was the one who continued to push and yell until Kade snapped. Besides, he'd actually hit Kade first. His opponent was just better at it than he was.

Kade pulled the Harley under the awning of the emergency department. "I'll get parked and be in," he said.

"Okay." Sam climbed off and started to head towards the automatic doors.

"Hey, Sam."

He turned around and looked at Kade. "Yeah?"

"Sorry."

Sam felt tears sting his eyes at the pain in the big man's voice. Without thought, he walked over to Kade and hugged him. "It's okay. I don't blame you."

"I blame myself. You'd better get inside and get yourself looked at."

Sam watched as Kade started the bike and pulled away. Hopefully Lark could help bring Kade out of his mood.

* * * *

Once released, the nurse wheeled Sam out of the exam room to the lobby. He was surprised to see Jack and Charlie sitting with Lark. "Where's Kade?"

Lark sighed. "He left about ten minutes ago after Charlie and Jack got here."

"Why are you here?" Sam asked Charlie.

"The hospital called me. Said you'd need a ride home. You feel like talking about it?"

"Later." Sam turned to Jack. "Right now I need you to take me over to Jace's."

"The hell I will. That guys a loose canon," Jack grumbled.

"No he isn't. He's depressed and he needs a friend. His happens to be in London." The nurse over his shoulder cleared her throat. "Oh, sorry." He looked back to Jack. "Please take me to Jace's?"

Lark stood up. "I'll go in with him to make sure everything is okay."

Sam looked at Lark and smiled. Oh, ow, well, tried to smile. "Thanks."

"Don't mention it."

* * * *

Just as he and Lark had suspected, Kade was packing his bags. Kade looked over his
shoulder as they walked into the room. "You didn't have to bring reinforcements. I'm not gonna hit you again."

Carol Lynne

Sam started to say something, but Lark grabbed his arm. "Can I have a few minutes alone with Kade?"

"Sure," Sam said and walked out.

Going into the kitchen he looked through the fridge for something to fix for dinner. With little else on hand, Sam decided to make bacon, eggs and pancakes, comfort food.

As he bent over to get a skillet from under the counter, stars lit up his vision. He put his hand out to steady himself and barely made it to one of the island stools. "Shit," he said taking several deep breaths.

His cell phone buzzed and Sam closed his eyes. He knew it had to be Jace. Fumbling in his pocket, he pulled out his phone. "Hey."

"Are you ready for me?" Jace asked in his sexiest voice.

"Actually, I'm not feeling well this evening. I'm sorry. I know you were looking forward to it, and so was I, but my heart just wouldn't be in it."

Sam heard Jace move around. "What's wrong?"

He knew he'd have to tell him about his injury eventually, so he might as well get it over with. Of course he didn't plan on telling him how he got it. He wasn't that stupid. "I ran into a door and broke my nose." Sam winced. It was a stupid lie but it was all he could think of.

"Broke your nose? Did you go to the doctor? Are you sure it's broken?"

Sam grinned at Jace's apparent concern. "Definitely broken. It was kind of off to the right side of my face. I went to the emergency room and they reset it for me. The doctor said I should be fine, although I'll probably have a small crook in it. Not that my face was perfect before."

"Did they give you something for the pain?"

"Yeah, I was just getting ready to make me, Lark and Kade some bacon and eggs."

"Bullshit! You go lie down on my bed and tell Kade to make dinner," Jace said in a vehement tone Sam had never heard.

"I'll ask him."

"Put him on the phone and I'll tell him. I don't understand what he's thinking having you cook for him in your condition."

Sam sighed. "I can take care of it myself, Jace. I don't need you to go all Alpha male on me right now."

After several moments, Jace spoke. "I'm sorry. I just hate that I'm not there."

"I know. Call me in the morning. I'll probably skip class, so I should be available any time."

"Okay. Take care of yourself and I'll talk to you soon."

"Bye." Sam hung up. He looked at the clock and yawned. Standing, he went to the stove to start dinner.

Chapter Nine

Sam opened his eyes the following morning to the sun slipping through the blinds. He groaned and reached for the bottle of pain medicine on Jace's bedside table. After fumbling for a tablet, he noticed his water glass was completely empty. "Shit."

"You need something?"

Startled, Sam flipped over and quickly covered himself. "Morning, Kade. Would you get me a glass of water?"

Kade walked over and picked up the empty glass from the opposite side of the bed. "Jace is gonna kill me when he sees your face," he mumbled.

Sam's hands went to his taped nose. He could feel the swelling and imagined he had two black eyes. "I told him I ran into a door," Sam confessed.

Kade stopped in his tracks. "Why would you do that?" Kade shook his head vehemently. "You can't lie to him. Jace takes that kind of thing very seriously."

Sam sat up. "See that's the thing. It wasn't just your actions. I was as much to blame if not more, and the last thing I want is for you and Jace to fight over it."

Kade ducked into the adjoining bathroom. When he came back into the room he handed Sam the glass of water. Sitting on the bed, Kade seemed to study Sam. "You're a good man. But I still want you to tell Jace the truth."

Sam grinned. "Maybe I should dodge his calls for a few days."

"No. You should probably call him as soon as possible."

Kade stood and looked down at Sam. "I told Lark I'd take him back to BK. You want a ride?"

Sam glanced around the room. Even though it wasn't his, he felt comfortable right where he was. He knew Jace wouldn't mind if he hid out there for another day, and it might be good to keep an eye on Kade. "I'm pretty comfortable right where I am. I'll probably sleep most of the day anyway. Do you mind if I stay?"

"Not at all. Gets pretty quiet around here with Jace gone."

"Then it's settled."

* * * *

The ringing phone on the bedside table woke him from a sound sleep. Sam reached over without opening his eyes. "Hello," he mumbled.

"Sam?"

"Hey, Jace," Sam yawned.

"I've been trying to call your cell for hours."

Sam opened his eyes and looked around the room. "Sorry, I think I left my jeans in the bathroom. Phone's in the pocket." He cringed at his nasally voice.

"I was worried. How are you?"

"Sleepy. The pain meds seem to really knock me on my ass." Sam thought about what Kade had said earlier.

"Go back to sleep, baby. I'll call you later."

"No. Wait. I need to tell you something," Sam spit out.

"Okay. What's going on?"

Sam decided to start at the beginning and go from there. "Remember when you asked me to check on Kade?"

"Yeah."

"Well, when I got here, all the curtains were drawn and I could tell he hadn't bathed or shaved in several days. I asked him to dinner and he turned me down saying he didn't need a babysitter. I said a few things that weren't very nice and he fired back a few things. Like a kitten taking on a St. Bernard, I slapped him, and Kade retaliated with a well placed punch to my nose."

"What! I'll fucking kill him. After all I've done for him? That bastard," Jace continued to scream.

"Stop it, please, just stop," Sam pleaded. "Kade was no more to blame than me. He was ready to pack up and get down the road, but Lark and I talked him out of it. He feels terrible, Jace. Just let this one go."

It must have finally sunk in. "You lied to me," Jace whispered.

"Yes. I didn't want to come between you and Kade. Actually, Kade's the one who told me I had to be honest with you. I'm sorry."

"What else have you lied to me about?" Jace growled.

"Nothing. I promise."

Sam heard Jace's exaggerated sigh. "Look, I'll call you later. Give me some time to process what you've told me."

"I really am sorry," Sam said. He felt tears sting his eyes and quickly blinked them away.

"Bye, Sam." Jace hung up without giving him a chance to say goodbye.

Groaning, he hung up the phone. "I've really screwed up this time," he whispered.

* * * *

Two days later, Jace still hadn't called him back. Sam couldn't remember a time when he'd felt so low. He returned to classes among stares from his classmates, and finally went back to work.

Margaret at the front desk gasped when she saw him for the first time since his accident. Sam shrugged and kept going. He didn't feel like explaining his injury again. Everyone he met wanted to know what had happened. Jack had even asked him the evening before if he needed some self-defence lessons.

Sam just wanted it all to go away. Sitting at his desk, he looked at the stacked boxes. Why was it they all reminded him of Jace? He knew it was stupid, but just looking at the boxes made him want to break down.

What a turn his life had undergone. Now, instead of him trying to cheer up Kade, it had been the other way around.

He was finishing his second stack of files, when a knock sounded at the door. "Just a minute," he called. Walking over, he opened the door.

"Oh, shit, Margaret wasn't joking," Tony chuckled.

Sam rolled his eyes and turned back to his chair. "Can I help you with something?" he politely asked his boss.

"Yeah," Tony replied. He shut the door and leaned against a tower of boxes. "You can start by telling me what happened. Then I would very much like to know if this is the reason my new Vice-President asked for an extended vacation?"

Sam felt like he'd been punched in the gut. "How long of a vacation?"

"He'll be gone until mid-May. He said he wants to tour Spain, Italy and Greece while he's over there."

Quickly wiping away a tear that escaped, Sam looked down at the floor. "Just long enough for me to finish the semester and head home. You're right. It's all my fault." He went on to tell Tony about the disagreement with Kade that led to his broken nose as well as the lie he'd told Jace.

When he was finished, he wiped away a few more tears. "If this is what love feels like, you can keep it."

Tony walked over and squatted in front of Sam's chair. "So you do love him." It wasn't a question, more of a confirmation.

"Yeah, stupid me. I've tried calling him several times, but he won't answer."

Placing his hands on Sam's knees, Tony leaned forward until Sam finally looked up. "Unfortunately you've done almost the worst thing possible in Jace's eyes. When he was with Kade, he heard lies day in and day out. I honestly think in his mind, Kade was trying to save Jace the heartache. But the fact remained, he still lied. About stupid shit, too. He was afraid to tell Jace he was into the rougher stuff as far as sex was concerned, so he cheated. When he'd get home with bruises, he'd tell Jace he got into a fight, or fell off his motorcycle..."

"Or ran into a door," Sam interrupted. He looked Tony in the eyes. "I haven't cheated. I would never do that to him."

"I know. The problem is, he doesn't, and he's the one who'll have to figure that out."

"Maybe I should quit? That could be one of the reasons Jace asked for the time off."

Tony stood. "I'd really prefer you stayed. I was planning to ask you to work full-time over the summer. If Jace has a problem with you working here, he'll need to get over it."

"I'll think about it."

"Please, do." Tony gave Sam a quick hug and left.

* * * *

For another two days, Sam waited for a call. He'd finally promised Tony he'd work until the end of classes and then make his decision. Tony said he understood. They both knew everything depended on Jace.

He'd come to the realisation that if what he thought was happening really was, there would be no way he could continue to work for Bianchi Bytes.

It was past quitting time and Tony and Daniel had asked Sam to join them for dinner. He rode up the empty elevator and knocked on Tony's door.

"Come in," Tony called.

Sam opened the door and was surprised to see Tony was alone. "I thought Daniel was meeting us here?"

Tony started laughing. "Yeah, well he tends to lose track of time. I hope you don't mind if we run by the college and drag him from the studio?"

"No, not at all." Sam found his eyes wandering to Tony's phone. "Um...do you mind if I try to call Jace from your phone? He won't take my calls, but I really need to talk to him."

"Sorry, Sam, but I can't give you that kind of permission. That would feel like betraying a friend." Tony ran his hand through his hair and stood. Slipping on his suit jacket he turned to Sam. "I'm going to check out the building before we leave. Feel free to sit at my desk while I'm wandering. I should be back in about fifteen minutes."

Sam heard the message loud and clear. "Okay, I'm sure I'll find something to occupy my time."

He saw Tony grin as he exited the room. With the door closed, Sam picked up the office phone and punched in Jace's number. He knew it was late in London. Shit, it had to be around midnight.

Sam crossed his fingers.

Jace was in mid-laugh when he picked up the phone. He finished his conversation before he greeted his caller. "...save my place, Dave. I'll be right back. Hello?"

Sam froze, as his throat went dry. Feeling like ten kinds of fool, he quickly hung up.

Running out the door, he headed straight to the restroom where he proceeded to throw up. By the time he'd composed himself, he heard Tony calling for him. Sam wiped his face with a wet paper towel and looked at himself in the mirror. "You idiot. You've been mooning over someone you never really had."

Tony stuck his head in. "You ready?"

As Sam studied his reflection he knew he had two choices. He could sink into the pit of despair along side of Kade, or he could pull himself up and go on, even if it would be a charade.

"Yeah, I'm ready."

Chapter Ten

"So you really did it, huh?" Tony asked.

"Did what?" Jace zipped his suitcase and transferred the phone to his other ear.

"Broke up with Sam."

Jace released the suitcase and stood. "Not officially. I just need some time away. I told you that when I asked for the vacation. I'm headed to Athens this afternoon as a matter of fact."

"Is that what you told Sam last Friday? That you just needed a little time?"

Looking around the room for anything he'd forgotten, Jace shook his head. "Stop talking in circles. I haven't spoken to Sam in almost two weeks."

"Really? Because I know he called you last Friday night."

Jace suddenly remembered the phone call he'd received. If that was Sam, and he heard...

"Shit."

"Jace?"

"It's nothing. I got a call on the hotel phone, but the person hung up." Jace sat on the bed.

"Well, whether you broke it off or not, the vultures are circling. And I'd suggest you either get your ass back here and claim what's obviously yours, or let him go."

"Are you telling me he's already seeing other people?" The thought turned him cold.

"I don't think so, but he's changed in the past week. I can't really put my finger on it, but he seems kind of...hollow. It's like he's going through the motions but that's it. And there are definitely a few guys who're showing interest."

"Thanks for calling, Tony. If I don't get moving I'm gonna miss my flight."

Tony sighed into the phone. "You're making the mistake of a lifetime. See you when you get back." Tony hung up and Jace felt like throwing the phone across the room.

The thought of Sam kissing someone made him feel sick. On the other hand, the fact that Sam could kiss someone so soon after what they'd shared made him feel sick.

Even though the urge to fly back to the states was strong, Jace pushed it away. He decided he'd call Sam when he arrived in Athens. "Damn it!" he shouted to the empty room.

* * * *

"Come on, Lark, don't look at me that way," Sam whined as he put on his tightest pair of jeans. "It'll just be for a little while, I promise. I need to get out and forget about Jace, at least for one night."

Lark ran a brush through his hair. "I think it's a bad idea. You're too on edge lately. I never know if I should duck or give you a hug when you walk into the room."

Sam caught a glimpse of himself in the mirror. Yeah, he'd definitely changed. A broken heart tended to do that to a person. He thought about the call he'd received from Jace earlier in the day. When Jace's name flashed on his display, Sam had automatically hit the off button. He hadn't the heart to talk to him. He knew Jace left a message, but he hadn't been up to listening to it yet.

What could his ex-lover have to say? Sorry, but I've found someone else? No, Sam knew he couldn't live through hearing that. Sitting on the bed, he pulled his cowboy boots on. He planned to do plenty of dancing and drinking in the next few hours.

"Ready?" he asked Lark.

Lark rolled his eyes. "I've never been to a place like this. What if they laugh at me? I mean, look at me. I don't belong in a place like Lucky's."

Sam studied his friend and roommate. "Mind if I help?"

"Help what?" Lark asked, taking a step back.

Reaching out, Sam took off Lark's glasses. "Wow. Your eyes are amazing without these covering them. Do you have to wear them to see everyday stuff?"

Lark shook his head. "They're more like reading glasses, but I've worn them so long I feel naked without them."

"Let's leave them at home for one night. Now, about your hair…"

* * * *

As soon as they walked into the bar, Sam grinned. Yep, this was just what he needed. He and Lark were already gathering interest, and they hadn't even sat down. He looked over his shoulder at his friend. "Come on. I see an empty table."

Lark took a seat across from him and Sam shook his head. "I still can't believe the transformation. You're hot," he chuckled.

Lark scowled and adjusted his shirt. "I can't believe you destroyed my clothes."

Sam grinned. He'd taken an old pair of Lark's jeans and cut strategic holes in them to show off his best feature, his ass. The shirt had been easy to modify. Sam had simply cut off the arms and some of the length, leaving enough to tempt men with the site of Lark's pierced belly button. Who on earth would think a nerd like Lark would have piercings?

When Sam had questioned him, Lark told him he was raised in a very open and free environment. He didn't go into details and Sam didn't ask. Obviously it was a sensitive subject.

After downing his first shot of whiskey, Sam started to feel more comfortable. Whiskey did it to him every time. He had two more shot glasses in front of him and reached for his second of the night.

"Don't you think you should slow down?" Lark asked, sipping his hard cider.

"No, not really. I'm here to forget. What better way?" Sam tipped the tiny glass and let the light brown liquor slide down his throat. He hated the taste and it burned like hell, but it seemed to be doing its job.

A good-looking man walked up to their table and seemed to study them both. "Either of you care to dance?"

"Sure," he replied and slid out of the booth. "I'm Sam," he said as he led the way to the dance floor.

"I'm Christian," the blond Adonis whispered in his ear.

Sam turned and was immediately enveloped in the much bigger man's arms. "Nice to meet you, Christian."

As they moved to the music, Sam could feel the alcohol quickly moving through his system. He closed his eyes and pretended his dance partner had dark brown hair and deep brown eyes.

Sam didn't know how many songs they'd danced to, but they'd taken a break to drink a few more shots. Lark had tried to get him to leave after his fifth drink, but Sam was feeling no pain and had refused.

So far, Christian had been fairly harmless. His hands had roamed Sam's body, but when the big man tried to kiss him, all it took was a no, for Christian to retreat.

He needed this, to be held, touched, even if by a stranger. At least he felt something other than heartache.

"I think it's time to get you home," a deep voice said from over his shoulder.

Sam tried to look behind him and started to fall. Damn, he guessed he was a little drunker than he'd thought.

Kade's strong arms caught him before he fell on his face. For a moment there seemed to be a sort of power struggle between the two men. When Sam heard another voice enter the foray, he struggled to concentrate. He knew that voice.

Tony was chest to chest with Christian, as Kade easily swung Sam into his arms. "So sleepy," he mumbled against Kade's chest.

"I'll get you home, Sammy."

As Kade started weaving through the crowd,

Sam felt the room begin to spin. "I think I'm gonna be sick," he panted, drawing in deep breaths.

"Lark!" He heard Kade yell. "Bathroom, now."

He felt his stomach tighten as the bile rose. "Gonna," he managed as Kade pushed through the bathroom door.

"Get lost," Kade said to a couple in one of the stalls. Kade set him in front of the stool as Sam began to throw up.

Kade held Sam's hair back with one hand, as he kept him from falling over with the other.

He felt a cold paper towel land on his forehead as the last of the undigested alcohol left his stomach. "God I'm never drinking again," he whined.

"That's what they all say," Kade chuckled.

Sam looked up into Lark's concerned face. "Something to wipe my mouth."

Kade took over holding the paper towel to his forehead as Lark retrieved another one for Sam's mouth. "Thanks."

"I hope you're not mad I called Kade. I knew you didn't know what you were doing and I wasn't big enough to get you to leave."

All Sam could manage was a grunt, but he patted Lark's foot.

"Are you sure you're finished?" Kade asked.

"Mmm hmm." He was quickly picked back up into Kade's arms. Closing his eyes, Sam drifted as Kade carried him out of the bar.

They stopped moving and Sam heard other voices join them. He managed to open his eyes. Tony and Daniel were looking at Sam with worried expressions. "I thought I saw you," Sam mumbled.

Tony opened the back door of his sedan. "We were having dinner with Kade when he got the call."

Kade climbed into the backseat still holding Sam. "Lark?" Sam asked.

"Right here," his friend said, getting in the other side of the car.

"You're nice."

"Keep telling yourself that. I don't really want a fat lip in the morning when you remember I called in reinforcements."

Sam felt a rumble against his cheek as Kade growled. "I won't let him touch you," Kade said to Lark.

Sam smiled. "Isn't Lark hot, Kade?"

"You're drunk," Kade replied. "You'd better shut up before you say something you regret."

Sam felt the car pull out of the lot. "You taking me home?"

"Yeah," Tony said from the driver's seat.

"I wish Jace's house was my home," he mumbled. "He doesn't want me anymore." Sam felt himself starting to drift again. "He already replaced me."

* * * *

After they got Sam to bed, they sat around the living room. Tony looked at the clock. "I think we should call Jace."

Lark shook his head. "Sam would kill us."

"I've already told you, no one's going to touch you," Kade grumbled.

Tony couldn't help but notice the looks flying between Lark and Kade. Interesting. "Have you talked to him since he's been gone?" he asked Kade.

"I tried once. He told me to stay out of his personal life. It's the push I needed to start working again, though. I've got to get a place of my own before he comes back to town."

"Wow, so you're working again?" Tony couldn't believe it.

"Not yet, but I'll find something."

"So you're staying in Idaho?" Lark asked. Tony could see the hope in the small man's eyes.

"For a while, I guess."

Tony cleared his throat. "Back to Jace and Sam. The problem as I see it is neither of them trusts the other. Jace's been hurt before and doesn't want to go down that same road, and Sam thinks Jace cheated on him in London."

He looked around the room to make sure everyone was following him so far. "The first thing we need to do is ask Jace if he slept with someone else. If the answer is yes, then we band together and get Sam through this."

"It doesn't sound like Jace. Even if he had given up on a relationship with Sam, I don't think he'd be jumping into the fire so soon," Kade remarked.

Tony pulled out his cell phone. "There's only one way to find out. Are we all in agreement?"

"He may never speak to us again," Daniel replied.

"You're right. That's why I'm asking." The four of them looked at each other before nodding their agreement.

Chapter Eleven

Sam carefully stepped into the kitchen, making sure not to make any noise. He raised a hand to Jack and put his fingers to his lips.

Jack chuckled as Sam sat at the island. Turning his back on him, Jack pulled several items out of the fridge and cupboards. Within minutes a red concoction was set in front of him. "Drink it," Jack ordered.

The smell alone was enough to make Sam's stomach roll. He made a face and pushed the glass away. "Can I just have some aspirin?"

"That'll do you more good than aspirin. That remedy has kept more than one marine from missing drills. Now drink."

Sam picked up the glass more to shut Jack up than anything. Holding his nose, he took his first sip and grimaced.

"Don't taste it, swallow it." He was once again ordered.

Taking a deep breath, Sam chugged the rest of the nasty drink. When he was finished, he ran to the sink afraid it wouldn't stay down. He heard Jack start to chuckle again.

After several minutes, Sam turned away from the sink. "Can I have some aspirin now?"

Jack pointed towards the cupboard. "Help yourself. By the way, some guy named Christian called for you earlier."

"Christian?" Sam searched his memory as he shook out three tablets.

"He said he met you at Lucky's and you mentioned where you lived. Probably not a smart idea if you're going to get so shit faced."

Sam gave Jack a slight wave. "Thanks for the remedy. I'm gonna go die now." He made his way back to his room and shed his clothes once more. He wasn't sure who'd undressed him the previous night. Hell, he wasn't even sure how he'd made it home. He'd yet to see Lark.

Remembering the transformation he'd done on Lark brought a smile to his face. Who knew his roommate was such a sexy little thing. He wondered if Lark had gotten any action.

Covering his head with the sheet, Sam let himself fall back into the land of dreams. Maybe if he was lucky, he'd have another one about Jace.

* * * *

Sam ran passed Margaret the following Monday afternoon. "Can't talk, I'm late."

Margaret giggled and waived.

Quickly punching in his pass code, Sam opened the door to his small makeshift office. He grabbed his chest as he was greeted by the man sitting in his chair.

"Hello, Sam."

"Jace. What are you doing back?" Sam felt frozen to the spot. He could tell Jace had picked up some sun wherever he'd spent the past several days.

"I arrived last night. I thought you might let me take you to dinner this evening." Jace narrowed his eyes. "Unless of course you have other plans."

"No. I mean I don't have plans, but I'm not sure about dinner." Sam crossed his arms. "How's Dave?"

Jace glanced at his watch. "He should be just finishing up dinner with his wife and children." He looked back at Sam. "When you called my hotel, several of us were playing poker. That's all."

"Really," Sam replied. He wasn't sure if he believed Jace. He wanted to, oh god he wanted to, but too much had happened since Jace had left for London.

Jace stood and slowly walked towards him. "Yes, really." Jace ran his long slender finger down the bridge of Sam's nose. "Almost healed," he whispered.

"Yeah, a couple of weeks will do that." Sam pulled back, away from Jace's electrifying touch.

"I need to tell you something. I went out and got wasted a couple of days ago. Nothing happened, but I danced with some guy. I wouldn't let him kiss me though."

"Yes, I know. You danced with Christian Foster. He's a grade A prick. He used to have my job and a spot in Tony's bed until he fucked them both up."

Sam just stood there unsure of what to say.

"Have dinner with me. I need to explain a few things."

Suddenly, out of nowhere, Sam felt angry. He'd suffered for the past two weeks and Jace waltzes in and expects to just explain his way out of it. With his hands balling into fists he turned his back. "I don't think I need to hear your explanation. I lied to you to keep two old friends from fighting. I know about your past with Kade and what he did, but if you can't tell the difference between him and me, I've nothing to say to you."

Jace put his hand on Sam's shoulder, and he whirled around. "Don't. You've put me through pure hell. You didn't call, you wouldn't take mine. Goddamit, Jace. I loved you. I would've done absolutely anything for you."

Jace looked stunned. "You love me?"

"I said loved. I'm not sure what I feel anymore." Sam shook his head and opened the door. "I gave you my heart once, and you didn't take very good care of it. I'm not sure I can do it again."

Without waiting for a reply, Sam walked out. He was almost to the bus stop when he heard Jace shouting his name. He glanced over his shoulder at Jace's sleek Jaguar.

"Please, get in," Jace pleaded.

Sam stopped and put his hands on his hips. He knew what would happen if he got in Jace's car. Despite everything, he knew he still loved the bastard. It was clear they both had trust issues that needed work if they were ever going to make a relationship work.

With a sigh, Sam walked towards the driver's window and bent down. "I don't want to fight with you." Sam looked around the parking lot. "I'm so tired of feeling like a walking corpse."

"Get in, baby. Let me take care of you," Jace whispered.

"I don't need you to take care of me. I just need you to love me." Sam felt the sting of tears and quickly blinked them away.

"Lucky for us, I want to do both." Jace leaned over the console and opened the passenger door, looking back at Sam, imploring him to take another chance.

Going around, Sam got in. The feel of warm leather felt somehow comforting as he shut the door. "Where are we going?"

"I don't care as long as we're together. We could go back to my place."

Sam shook his head. "Maybe the lake would be a good idea."

Jace cupped Sam's cheek. "I have a blanket in the trunk. Should we get stuff for a picnic lunch?"

Sam nodded. "I haven't eaten much lately."

"I can tell." Jace traced the dark circles under Sam's eyes. He leaned forward and placed a kiss on Sam's forehead. "I'm sorry."

* * * *

Sam stretched as the warm afternoon sun bathed his skin. He opened his eyes and yawned. "Sorry, how long have I been asleep?"

Jace grinned. He was on his side with his head propped on his hand looking down at Sam. "A little over an hour." He ran a hand over Sam's bare chest. "You're starting to get a little pink though."

Sam revelled in the touch. They'd spent a great deal of time talking while they ate and relaxed beside the crystal clear water. He wasn't sure when he'd fallen asleep, but Jace didn't appear to be upset with him.

He'd promised to never lie to Jace again. Even if he thought it would spare Jace's feelings from getting hurt. Jace promised to work on his trust issues, and that was enough for Sam, at least for now.

Jace's thumb circled Sam's light brown nipple. "I've missed you," Jace said as he descended. A warm tongue traced a

91

path from under Sam's arm to the pebbled nub. Teeth scraped across the sensitive skin as Jace groaned.

Hard and wanting, Sam thrust his hips against Jace's thigh. Pulling off his nipple, Jace looked around. They still appeared to be the only ones playing hooky. "What do you want, baby?"

"Your mouth. Oh god I want to feel your mouth on me," Sam moaned, threading his fingers through Jace's dark hair.

Repositioning himself, Jace licked his way down Sam's torso. Sam quickly unzipped his jeans and pushed them and his underwear down as far as he could in his present position.

Bypassing his cock, Jace nuzzled his nose against Sam's heavy sac. Short teasing licks were given but no relief was in sight. "Please," Sam begged.

Looking around once more, Jace pulled Sam's clothes completely off and flung them to the side. Straddling Sam's legs, Jace leaned forward and took the head of Sam's cock into his mouth. "Yessss," Sam hissed.

Jace pumped up and down on Sam's cock a few times before releasing it. Sam groaned in frustration, but Jace merely chuckled, "Patience, baby."

Sliding his body down Sam's legs, Jace repositioned them. With his legs bent and open wide, Sam was fully exposed to Jace's lustful gaze. "I don't know where to begin," Jace said.

"Anywhere," Sam groaned, "just somewhere."

Grinning, Jace licked his way around Sam's balls, sucking one and then the next into his mouth. Sam gripped the blanket on either side of him and drew his knees to his chest. "More," he croaked.

"Mmm hmm." Jace moved down to bury his face in the crack of Sam's ass, inhaling deeply. The slick tongue working around his hole had Sam on edge in no time.

Jace introduced a finger, lubing the pucker with spit as he pushed another in. "Need you," Jace murmured.

"Yes." Sam turned over and got on his hands and knees.

Jace knelt behind him and unzipped his dress slacks, allowing his cock to spring free. He spit several times into his hands and lubed his cock. "It's gonna be down and dirty, baby."

"Sounds good to me," Sam said, grabbing his own cock.

The blunt head of Jace's cock pressed against his hole, finally pushing passed the first ring of muscles. They rocked back and forth in unison until Jace was buried to the hilt.

"Missed you," Jace growled as he slowly pulled out and slammed back in. The faster the pace, the more Jace babbled. "Missed your smile, your laugh, and this ass. Never had an ass like yours, never. It hurt, hurt when you lied. I thought I'd lost you forever."

"Never," Sam answered back. "Never gonna lose me."

Jace bent and bit Sam's back, soothing it with his tongue. "Come for me. Come with my cock buried inside of you."

The next bite was even more intense, and Sam grunted as he spilled his seed on the blanket below. Who knew he liked to be bit? He hoped they explored this new development further in the future.

Jace bit Sam one last time on the shoulder as he pumped him full of cum. His teeth were still firmly embedded in Sam's flesh as he shook with the aftershocks.

They both collapsed on the blanket and Jace began soothing the mark with his tongue. "Did I hurt you?" Jace panted.

Sam was a little embarrassed to admit that he liked it, but he promised to be truthful. "It was hotter than fuck. You can bite me anytime."

Jace rolled off Sam's back and turned him over. "Really?"

"God yes."

"I can see a lot of bruises in your future." Jace replied, nipping at Sam's nipple.

Sam squirmed, feeling his cock begin to harden. "Take me to dinner and then I'll let you feast on me all you want."

Jace grinned and sat up. "Where would you like to dine, Mr. Howard?"

Sam watched as Jace tucked his half-hard cock back into the charcoal grey dress slacks. "I don't care as long as it's on the way."

"The Grog and Galley is just down the road." Jace ran a finger down Sam's bare chest. "You'll need protein to keep up with me."

"Mmm, I guess you'll need to fill me with plenty of it." Sam winked.

Jace chuckled and stood. "Come on, tease, let's get out of here."

* * * *

They were in the middle of thick juicy filets when Sam caught him staring. "What?"

Jace shook his head, and took another bite. "You amaze me."

"Me? I'm nothing special." Sam wiped his mouth and took a drink of his water.

Jace ran his foot up the inside of Sam's calf. "I beg to differ."

Sam blushed. "Is this about the whole biting thing? Because until you did it, I never knew what a turn-on it was."

"I've always had a thing for biting, even as a child. I've just never had a lover who enjoyed it. Usually complaints follow a fuck like the one we had." Jace took a sip of wine. "It's not just that though, it's everything. We really are suited for one another."

Sam looked at him with such heat in his eyes Jace felt it in his groin. "Eat up. We've got a lot of making up to do."

"Sam?" A smooth voice said from behind Jace.

The hair on the back of Jace's neck prickled. He knew that voice. Standing, Jace turned around to face Christian. "Get lost."

Christian had the nerve to grin. "I don't believe I was talking to you. I've been trying to get this young man on the phone for several days now. I guess its fate we're both here."

"Listen, Christian…"

Jace cut Sam off. "If you ever try to contact Sam again, I'll kill you. Better yet, I'll sic Kade on you."

"I'm not afraid of you or that tattooed freak."

"I'm not interested, Christian," Sam said, coming to wrap an arm around Jace's waist. "We danced, that's all. I don't want anything you have to offer."

"You will," Christian smirked. "Jace will be playing the field before you know it and you'll be left alone, again."

Jace started to lunge for the big asshole, but Sam tightened his grip. "Don't, Jace. He's not worth it."

Christian chuckled and turned away. "Call me, Sam."

If he didn't know Christian as well as he did, he would've taken him seriously. Despite his bluster, Jace knew Kade scared the crap out of Christian, he always had.

"Let's go home," Sam whispered. "We've had a wonderful day. Don't let that scum ruin it."

Jace turned back to Sam and kissed his forehead. "Okay, baby."

Chapter Twelve

Kade was stretched out on the couch when they arrived at Jace's house. It was the first time Sam had seen the big man without a shirt. Damn. He'd never seen so many tattoos. He grinned at the gold hoops through Kade's nipples. They were big, but not nearly as big as Lark's.

Jace caught Sam staring and growled. Sam looked up at Jace and grinned. He turned back to Kade. "Have you ever seen Lark's piercings?"

Kade's eyes rounded like a deer caught in the headlights. "Why would I have seen Lark's? Well, okay, I take that back. I did see the pretty one in his belly button when you dressed him up the other night, but that's it."

Deciding to push, Sam took a step forward. "And what did you think of the way he was dressed?"

A far away look passed over Kade's face for a moment. "I think he'll get himself in trouble if he goes out like that again."

"From you or someone else?" Sam chuckled.

Kade grunted and left the room. Jace kissed the top of Sam's head. "You seem to have hit a sore spot."

"Good."

"Just remember what I told you about Kade. He's very adamant about never having sex again. I guess it's his way of paying for his sins."

Sam rolled his eyes. "He needs to get back into the land of the living. All I know is after the night Kade rescued me from the bar, Lark's been different. He stares off into space all the time and I've actually heard him jacking off during the night. Not good."

Jace lifted Sam's hand to his mouth. Sam thought he was about to bestow a kiss, but instead, Jace bit the fleshy part under his thumb. Sam felt his cock twitch.

"What about you?" Jace asked, releasing Sam's flesh. "Have you been getting yourself off at night?"

Sam turned to face Jace. He began unbuttoning the white dress shirt, licking a path as he did. "No, I prefer to do that in the shower." He bit Jace's uncovered nipple. "And I had to take a lot of showers."

Jace moaned and guided Sam's mouth to his other nipple. As Sam latched on using tongue and teeth, Jace went to work on the rest of their clothes. Before either of them knew it, they were both standing in the middle of the living room naked.

Sam fell to his knees and took Jace's cock into his mouth. He noticed Jace groaned every time he scraped the sensitive flesh with his teeth. Who knew it was something they had in common?

Jace spread his legs, and Sam moved down to his balls. He nudged Jace towards the sofa, needing more access. Taking the hint, Jace walked the few steps and positioned his knees on the cushion, resting his head and arms on the back of the couch.

"Mmm," Sam moaned. He reached out and ran his short nails down Jace's back as he licked at the puckered hole.

"Oh, fuck yeah," Jace growled.

"You like that?"

"You have no idea."

Sam gave Jace's ass cheek several good bites, enjoying the groans of pleasure he received.

"Oh fuck, you found someone into the same kinky shit as you," Kade said from behind Sam.

Jace turned quickly almost breaking Sam's nose again in the process. In one fluid motion, he grabbed the lap blanket from the couch and threw it over Sam's naked body. "Dammit, Kade. Can't we have a little privacy?"

Kade chuckled and continued to walk through towards the kitchen. "I'm just saying, the two of you are a match made in heaven. Nice ass by the way," he said to Sam as he passed.

"Keep your damn eyes off his ass," Jace bellowed.

Kade walked into the other room, but Sam
could still hear him laughing. "Hard to miss something like that when it's staring you right in the face," Kade yelled.

Sam was mortified and buried his head under the blanket. Jace picked him up and started carrying him to what Sam assumed was the bedroom.

"Don't worry about him, baby. He's seen and done a hell of a lot worse."

* * * *

Jace dropped him off at BK before heading to work the following morning. Sam tried to remember if he'd gotten his work done for class as he undressed. He'd already showered that morning with Jace, so maybe if he changed quickly he'd have time to go over his notes.

Sam was just slipping on a clean pair of briefs when he heard the door open.

"Oh my god, what happened to you?" Lark asked rushing to Sam's side.

Sam looked at him like he was crazy. "I made up with Jace. Sorry I didn't call."

Lark shook his head and waived his hands. "Not that. I figured that part out. I'm talking about the bruises."

Oh shit, he'd forgotten. Sam looked down at his bare chest. It was covered with small bruises and bite marks. Just the site of them started to turn him on. Sam turned away from Lark and pulled his shirt on. "Sorry, it's a…sexual thing." Geeze, he couldn't believe he was telling Lark about his new-found kink.

Lark whistled. "Better you than me." Lark started gathering his books.

Sam looked over his shoulder. "That's it?

You don't want to tell me how sick I am?"

Lark shrugged. "Why would I? It's your body."

Sam shook his head. "You amaze me sometimes. When I first met you I thought you were a nerd. Then I helped uncover your inner vixen, and now I find out you're open to kinky sex."

"I never said I was open to it. I just said what you do with your body is your business. Live and let live, ya know?"

Sam pulled a clean pair of jeans on before sitting on the bed. He grabbed his socks and studied Lark. "Can I ask you a personal question?"

"Sure." Lark sat across from him.

"Would you ever date someone with HIV?"

Lark looked like Sam had knocked the breath out of him. He slowly stood and picked up his pack. "HIV doesn't scare me, but ignorance does." Lark turned and walked out of the room without another word.

Sam scratched his head wondering what he'd said wrong.

* * * *

After dropping a file off at Tony's office, Sam decided to take a chance and see if Jace was in. His secretary, Ellen, told him Jace was on the phone but it should be okay for him to go on in. She even gave him a wink.

Shit. Did that mean Ellen knew about them? He thought they'd kept a pretty good lid on it at work. After giving Ellen an uncomfortable smile, he quietly stepped into Jace's office.

Jace grinned as soon as he spotted Sam and motioned him over. Sam started to take a seat in front of the big mahogany desk, but Jace snapped his fingers to get Sam's attention.

Jace motioned Sam closer, and he shook his head. He knew if someone walked in they'd get into a hell of a lot of trouble. Jace continued to beckon Sam over, giving him the signal to lock the door.

Lock the door? Wouldn't Ellen hear it engage? Still, his lover didn't seem too worried about anyone finding out, so Sam quietly did what he was supposed to. After securing the door, he walked to Jace's side and was immediately pulled into the lap he loved so much.

Jace had been insatiable since they got back together. Sam hadn't complained, nor would he, but damn.

A warm hand found its way under his sport shirt, petting his stomach and chest before squeezing his nipple. Sam felt his cock thicken inside his khakis. Jace continued to torment his bruised nipples as he carried on with what sounded like an overseas call.

Turning slightly, Sam began kissing Jace's neck as he unbuttoned his shirt. Thank god Jace didn't make it a practice to wear ties. In no time, Sam had Jace bared down the middle. He feasted his eyes on the bronze skin. He knew some of Jace's colouring was natural, but he still had some tan from his brief stay in Greece.

He found a dark bruise on Jace's neck, just below the collar, and licked it, scraping his teeth across the purple skin. Jace slid his hand down Sam's chest to unzip his khakis.

When Sam felt Jace wrap his fingers around

his erection, he moaned. Startled that he'd done it out loud, Sam covered his mouth and gave Jace an apologetic smile. Jace answered him by quickly winding up his call and hanging up.

"Trying to get me in trouble?" Jace teased.

"You're the troublemaker. I would've been perfectly content to snatch a quick kiss and go back to my office."

Jace applied more pressure to Sam's cock. "Really? And what about this?"

Sam thrust against Jace's fist. "I didn't have that when I walked in."

"Lucky you. I've been half-hard all day, which is why I've stayed at my desk. No sense frightening the natives."

Sam wiggled around on Jace's lap. "What would you like me to do about this little problem?"

Jace's phone took that moment to beep. Ellen's voice sounded over the intercom. "I'm sorry, Mr. Rawlings, but Tony's called an emergency meeting of all the department heads. He'd like for you to join them in the conference room."

"Thanks, Ellen, I'll be right there." The intercom clicked off and Jace groaned. "How in the hell am I supposed to walk into a meeting like this?"

Sam stood and looked down at Jace's cock pressing against the front of his dress slacks. "Give me two minutes." Sam quickly unzipped Jace and released his cock. Wasting no time, he swallowed as much of Jace's length as he could and bit down, not enough to break the skin, but enough to leave marks.

"Fuck!" Jace growled. He wrapped his fingers in Sam's curls and humped his face for several moments, before he tipped over the edge. Sam tasted the salty goodness coating the inside of his mouth and running down his throat.

As soon as he had Jace cleaned and tucked back in, he stood. Jace pulled him into a deep kiss and ran his palm over Sam's still hard cock. "What about you?"

"Don't worry about me. I'm young, people expect me to walk around with a hard-on," he said with a grin. Jace looked around on his desk and picked up a large red file folder.

"Here, carry this in front of you. I don't like the thought of anyone else looking at your cock, even if it is expected."

Sam shrugged and took the folder. He gave Jace a quick kiss and headed for the door. "By the way, when you're in your meeting, imagine me down in my office with one hand on my cock and the other in my ass."

Sam laughed as Jace groaned. He glanced at his man's trousers. He was sure Jace would be hard again as soon as his cock recovered. With a wave, he walked out the door, nodding to Ellen as he passed.

Chapter Thirteen

Sam was jonesing. He hadn't seen Jace for almost five days all because Jace insisted he study for his finals. Well, he was finally finished with the last of them and headed home to change. Jace had promised to pick him up at exactly three o'clock. At the rate he was going, he'd be lucky to get a shower first.

Stepping into the dorm, he heard a god-awful commotion coming from the kitchen. He looked at his watch and decided to take a shower before investigating. He knew it wasn't the responsible thing to do, but then he'd been five entire days without sex and a fight between Charlie and Jack wasn't his top priority.

Lark was sitting on the bed studying when he walked in. "Hey," Sam greeted his roommate.

"Hi," Lark said and went back to his books.

Things hadn't been the same since Sam had asked the all important question. He'd tried several times to apologise, but Lark always brushed him off.

"Are you done with finals?" Sam asked as he stripped down.

"One more at nine a.m.," Lark answered back.

"So, uh, you sticking around this summer?" Sam grabbed his towel and wrapped it around his waist.

"I'm not sure yet." Lark finally looked up. "You?"

"Yeah. I'm going to work full-time for Tony. I think I'll be staying at Jace's house to save up money."

Lark nodded. "Charlie said I can stay until the end of the month without paying for the summer session. Hopefully I'll be able to figure out what I'm doing before then."

"Look, uh, I gotta hop in the shower before Jace gets here, but I'd like to take you to lunch after your final. Sound good?"

"Sure."

"Great." Sam picked up his shower bucket and headed towards the bathroom.

* * * *

Hopping down the stairs, Sam met Liam on his way up. "Careful, it's a war zone down there," Liam commented.

"They still at it?"

"Yep. Are you coming to Nate's graduation party on Saturday?"

"Wouldn't miss it. You gonna be around until then?"

"Yeah, we don't move into the apartment until next week."

"Cool."

Sam heard what sounded like a pot being tossed across the kitchen. "I gotta find out what they're fighting over this time."

"Good luck," Liam grinned and continued up the stairs.

Jace walked in as Sam reached the bottom. "Hey, you." He ran and jumped into Jace's arms. The kiss they shared felt like the best of his life, Jace's tongue tangling with his. "I've missed you. Talking on the phone isn't the same."

Another loud crash sounded and Jace jumped. "What the hell is going on in there?"

"I don't know, but I was about to go find out. Wanna come?" Sam unwrapped his legs from around Jace's waist and stood.

"Not without another kiss to tide me over."

"My pleasure," Sam murmured against Jace's lips.

Once they broke apart, Sam led Jace by the hand towards the kitchen. "At least they've stopped throwing things."

Sam went first, pushing the swinging door open a crack. The sight that met him had Sam pulling back. "Okay, let's go."

"Wait. What's going on?"

Sam chuckled and quickly walked to the front door with Jace on his heels. "Let's just say, I hope they wash that counter before Jack prepares any more food."

Jace's brows shot up. "Really? They finally lit the match?"

"From what I saw, more like a stick of dynamite."

Jace looked back towards the kitchen. "Go, Charlie," he laughed.

* * * *

Jace parked next to a small cabin overlooking the lake. "Here we are."

105

Sam looked out his window and then back to Jace. "Do you know someone who lives here?"

"Yeah, us. I rented it for the summer." Leaning over, he gave Sam a kiss. "Come on, I want you to see the inside."

Stepping into the cabin, Jace waited for Sam's reaction. It didn't take long, the cabin was amazing.

"Holy crap." Sam walked straight through to the wall of windows at the back of the open floor plan.

"That was my reaction when I first looked at it. Amazing isn't it?" The entire house was bathed in light from the floor to ceiling windows, but the best part was the view. Looking out over one of the clearest lakes in Idaho, it gave the impression you were actually standing on the water.

Sam spun and walked into Jace's arms. "I love it. I still can't believe we get to live like this for an entire summer with no Kade."

Jace ran his cheek down the side of Sam's face before moving over to capture his lips. He pushed in deep, tasting his one and only. His hands landed on Sam's sweet ass and pulled him even closer. "I was thinking of buying it.

It's not practical during the winter months to drive back and forth to school and the office, but weekends could be ours."

"Naked," Sam said and started undressing.

The cabin was in a heavily wooded area with no close neighbours. "Yep, naked," Jace agreed and started taking his clothes off. "It's one of the things that sold me on this place. Unless you're on the water, no one can see us. I think naked should be the dress code while we're here."

Sam was naked first and pressed himself against the warm glass. He was quite a sight to behold. "I can't wait to see you browned from head to toe."

The thought alone had Jace's cock filling. He looked at Sam's fading bruises. "I haven't taken proper care of you lately."

Nude, he pressed himself against Sam. His hand ran over the light green bruise around Sam's nipple. God he wanted to make love to his man, right here, right now, with the sun still high enough in the sky to create a halo effect around the gorgeous body in his arms.

He held up a finger. "Don't move." Sam captured the digit in his mouth and sucked.

"Not going anywhere."

Reluctantly, Jace pulled away and went to the alcove set off to the side of the main room. He'd been by earlier to stock the cabin with necessities, and lube was definitely a necessity.

Grabbing the bottle on the small bedside table, Jace lubed his cock as he walked towards his sun god. He knew it would be a fast fuck, but it had been too long since he'd been inside Sam's heat.

Without preamble, Jace reached Sam and hoisted him up. Sam's legs wrapped around his waist and Jace used the remaining slick on his fingers to rim his lover's hole.

Positioning his cock, Jace looked into Sam's eyes. "Ready, or do you need stretching?" He knew his man. Jace could feel the already stretched hole trying to suck him in.

"Took care of that in the shower. Need you."

"Got me," he said impaling Sam.

"Uhhh," Sam moaned as Jace buried himself to the hilt.

Jace braced his arms under Sam's thighs and plunged in and out of his man. When a forceful stroke sent Sam's head hard against the glass, Jace stopped. "Shit."

He immediately pulled out and stood Sam on his feet. Feeling the back of Sam's head, he made sure he hadn't seriously injured his lover. "You okay, baby?"

Sam nodded and turned around, bracing his hands on the window sill. "Finish me."

As he pushed in, Jace bent over and dug his teeth into the soft flesh on Sam's shoulder blade. Jace's hips pistoned back and forth in an all out assault on Sam's ass, as he continued to bite and suck the tender skin.

"Yes," Sam cried as he painted the glass with his cum.

Jace felt like his cock was trapped in a vice as Sam's body contracted around him. "Oh fuck!" Jace howled as he emptied his seed deep into his love.

They both collapsed to the cool hardwood floor, curling around each other. "I love you," Jace panted. "I have for a long time."

Sam snuggled against Jace's side even more. "Is that why you reacted the way you did when I told you I'd lied?"

Sighing, Jace tilted Sam's chin up so he could look into his beautiful grey eyes. "I've never loved anyone who didn't lie to me. My parents lied to me for seventeen years."

Jace kissed Sam's forehead. He couldn't believe he was talking about this. He'd never told a soul about his parents, not even Kade.

"When I was a boy, I asked them why there weren't any baby pictures of me. They told an elaborate tale of how my baby album was ruined in a basement flood. When I was a senior in high school I was in a car wreck. My folks were brought into the emergency room and asked all kinds of questions. That's when I found out I'd been adopted when I was almost two-years-old. And I felt as though my entire life was a lie."

Sam ran his hand down Jace's chest. "Maybe they were trying to protect you?"

"Maybe. What they accomplished was to plant the seed of doubt in my mind. I mean, if you can't trust your parents to tell you the truth…"

He wiped the moisture from his eyes. "They'd lied to me for years and I never forgave them for it. Then Kade happened, and well, you know what went on with him."

"And you thought because I lied, I was just like them," Sam surmised.

"Yeah. Warning bells started going off in my head and I needed some time to weed through my feelings. I'm sorry I hurt you."

"It's in the past."

"I trust you. That's saying a lot for me."

"I'll never again give you a reason not to."

As the afternoon sun started to dip into the lake, Jace held onto his future. And Sam was his future, he knew that in his bones.

* * * *

Sam made it back to BK the following day in time to take Lark to lunch. He didn't know how to make it up to his friend, but he knew he needed to try.

When he didn't find Lark in their room, he went down to find Charlie who always knew where everyone was. "Hey, Jack, have you seen Charlie?"

"Why the hell would I know where Charlie is? I'm not his keeper," Jack barked.

Sam held up his hands. "Chill. I was just hoping he'd know where Lark is. I was supposed to take him to lunch but he's not around."

"Well if you have plans, I'm sure he'll be here. Now get out of my kitchen and leave me to my job."

Damn. Evidently Jack wasn't the type to walk around with post-sex afterglow. Sam grinned as he slumped on the couch. He wondered if Charlie was glowing,

Thirty minutes later, Lark walked in the front door.

"You ready?" Lark seemed a little out of it. Alarm bells started to ring in Sam's mind at Lark's odd behaviour. When they'd first started rooming together Lark had told him that he was diabetic, but so far he'd always seemed healthy. Sam tried to remember what Lark had told him about the symptoms of what did he call it, hypoglycaemia? "Lark? Are you okay?"

"Huh?"

He started walking up the stairs but seemed unsteady on his feet. Running up the steps, Sam put an arm around his friend.

He helped Lark sit on the bed and knelt in front of him. "Lark, do you have some candy or something you need to eat?"

Lark looked blank for several seconds before pointing to his desk drawer. Inside was a bag of Pixy Stix.

The door opened and Kade stepped inside holding a box. "Hey, Jace asked me to bring..." He seemed to notice Sam's panic. "What's wrong?"

"Lark's having some kind of hypoglycaemic attack. I need to get this candy in him."

Kade tossed the long box on the bed and knelt in front of Lark. "Hey, buddy, can you hear me?"

Lark blinked a couple of times but said nothing.

"He has some Pixy Stix. Do I just pour one into his mouth? What if he chokes?" Sam asked.

"Put it on his tongue and I'll help him close his mouth. Maybe get a glass of water and we can see if he can drink some of it."

Kade sat up on the bed next to Lark and wrapped one arm around him as he pried his jaws open. Sam ripped the top off the sugar-filled tube. He tapped the purple powder onto Lark's tongue.

Lark tried to fight, turning his head to the side, but Kade managed to get his mouth closed. "Water," Kade said.

Sam grabbed an empty glass from his desk and ran to the bathroom. He was back within seconds, handing the glass to Kade.

"Come on, Lark, I need you to take a few sips," Kade coaxed.

Sam's throat constricted at the gentle way Kade held Lark's small body in his arms. If those two didn't belong together he'd eat his hat. Kade held Lark while he started to come around.

Lark's eyes went wide as he realised someone was holding him. "What?"

"Shhh," Kade soothed.

Sam took the glass and set it on the desk. "You evidently haven't been taking care of yourself," Kade said. "We got some sugar into your system, but I think it would be a good idea to go to the emergency room and have you checked out."

Lark shook his head and tried to sit up. "I'm okay. I need to take my blood sugar level and eat something, but I'm fine now."

"Does that mean you're still interested in going to lunch?"

Lark nodded. "Give me a few minutes."

"Of course." Sam looked at Kade. He could see the worry written on his face. "Would you like to join us?"

Kade gazed at Lark for several seconds before shaking his head. "I need to get back to Bianchi. Tony gave me a job rewiring some of the offices. It'll work until I figure out what to do with my life."

Lark rested his hand on Kade's cheek and kissed him softly on the lips. "Thank you."

Kade jumped as if he'd been burned. "You're welcome." He released his hold on Lark and stood. "I'll, um, see you guys at the party."

"Thanks, Kade," Sam said as the big man walked out.

Sam looked at the forgotten white box. He walked over and opened it, smiling at the long stem roses inside. "I'm gonna go call Jace and thank him while you take care of your blood sugar."

"I'll be right down."

Sam opened the door and ran right into Kade. He quickly shut the door and put a hand on Kade's shoulder. "Are you okay?"

"He kissed me," Kade mumbled. "Doesn't he know?"

"No," Sam answered. "But I don't think it would make a difference. He likes you."

Kade ran his fingers through his long hair. "He's too sweet to deal with someone like me."

Sam grinned, thinking about the nights of listening to Lark jerk off. "You might be surprised."

Chapter Fourteen

Sam found Charlie in the kitchen. "Hey, you want a ride to Justin and Luc's?"

Charlie shook his head. "I don't think I'm going to go."

If he wasn't mistaken, it appeared as though Charlie had been crying. What in the hell could make the tougher than nails man shed tears? "Where's Jack?"

"Left," Charlie turned and started running soapy water into the sink. "He got a call earlier and flew out of here with no real explanation. Said hopefully he'd be back, and that's all."

Sam walked up behind Charlie and laid a hand on his shoulder. "I'm sorry. That sucks. I thought the two of you were finally starting to get along."

"Yeah, right," Charlie chuckled. "I guess I got along with Jack as well as anyone could. Didn't seem to matter much to him though, not with the way he shot out of here."

"Come to Bear's party."

Charlie reached back and covered Sam's hand with his own. "Thanks, but I need some time alone. Tell Bear I'm sorry I couldn't make it, and I'll catch up with him when he gets back from his folks."

"I will. Give me a holler if you feel like talking."

"Thanks, Sam."

Sam gave Charlie's shoulder one last squeeze before going out front to wait for Jace. He sat on the front step and thought of the people he cared about. His lunch with Lark had turned up an unexpected twist. And although he desperately wanted to talk to Kade about it, he was sworn to secrecy.

Jace gave a short toot of his horn as he pulled into the parking lot. "Hey, stud, can I give you a ride?"

Sam stood and walked towards the car. "Maybe later, but for now you can take me to a party." He got in and gave Jace a kiss.

"Charlie's not coming. Jack got a call and took off for who knows how long. Needless to say, Charlie's a little depressed."

"Maybe he'll change his mind and show up later," Jace put a hand on his thigh and pulled out of the parking lot. "So, do you know everyone that's going to be at Bear's party?"

"Not everyone. I haven't met Alec but Max seems nice. Most of the people that'll be there I know only casually. Is Kade coming?"

Jace gripped Sam's thigh momentarily. "Yeah. Why?"

Sam shrugged. "I'm sworn to secrecy." Sam chuckled and locked his mouth with an imaginary key. Boy would Kade be in for a surprise.

"You're keeping secrets from me?" Jace ran his hand up Sam's thigh to rub his balls. "I have ways of making you talk."

Sam spread his legs and allowed Jace to continue his delicious torture. "Lark's on the prowl," he finally blurted out, unzipping his shorts.

Jace wrapped his fingers around Sam's cock as he continued to drive. "Didn't you tell Lark he'd be wasting his time?"

"No. I've seen the way Kade looks at him. If anyone can bring Kade back into the land of the living it'll be Lark." Sam couldn't take it any more and pushed his shorts down to his knees. Scooting further down into the seat, he put his feet on the dash, exposing himself even more.

"Like that do you?" Jace released Sam's cock and put his middle finger into his mouth before inserting it into Sam's hole.

Panting, Sam grabbed his own cock and stroked himself to the rhythm pumping into his ass. "Oh fuck," he moaned as Jace inserted another finger.

"I love the way you always stretch yourself before we see each other. The image of you in the shower, fingering yourself…fuck."

Sam looked over at Jace's lap. The zipper on his shorts had to be digging in to that fat cock. Looking around, Sam motioned to a fairly empty parking lot. "Over there, park in back."

Jace did as instructed, driving to the far corner. As soon as the car stopped, Sam knelt on the seat and released Jace's cock. Wrapping his lips around the bulbous head, he bent forward, giving Jace his ass.

Two fingers plunged inside of him as he devoured Jace's beautiful cock. He rocked back and forth fucking himself on Jace's hand and in no time they were both coming. His ass clamped down as he heartily drank Jace's seed, his own splattering on the console.

Coming down, Sam laid his head in his lover's lap as he cleaned him up. When he sat up he looked down and laughed. "Sorry about that. Do you have any napkins in here?"

Jace shook his head, and bent to lick Sam's cum off the wood and leather console. "Damn that's hot," Sam groaned.

When Jace finished, he took a few licks of Sam's cock and then a deep kiss, sharing flavours. "You're hot," Jace said. "I've never been with anyone sexier."

Sam laughed and pulled up his shorts. "Yeah, right. Sorry if this hurts your feelings, but Kade's one hot motherfucker. Way hotter than me."

Jace started to shake his head, but Sam stopped him with a kiss. "But I like that you think I'm sexier."

* * * *

"Hey, guys," Luc greeted them as they carried their lawn chairs and cooler of beer to the backyard.

"Hi, Luc. Looks like you've got a good crowd here already," Jace said, looking around at the back yard.

"Yeah, well, Justin can't seem to stop himself when it comes to inviting friends over. Our group has gotten much bigger in the last year."

"Nothing wrong with that. Better to have too many friends than not enough."

"You said it. Try and find a spot to set up your chairs. I think we're still expecting a few more and you might as well save your space."

"Thanks, man," Jace said and led Sam over to a more secluded spot in the yard. It wasn't that he planned on being antisocial, he just knew his man. If the mood struck, Sam didn't seem to care much where he was.

Jace grinned, as Sam's hand brushed the front of his shorts as they set up their chairs. "Behave."

Sam winked. "We might need to take a trip to the restroom later. My hole is feeling awfully empty."

Jace groaned. He knew Sam was doing this on purpose. His lover enjoyed nothing more than teasing him with the forbidden fruit. "You're evil."

"And yours," Sam chuckled.

Jace gave Sam a deep, tongue fucking kiss. "Yeah, all mine."

"Break it up," Kade said walking towards them. He set his cooler down before spreading out a blanket.

"Uh, Kade? We chose this particular spot because of its privacy," Jace said, tapping Kade on the shoulder.

"Yeah, well, Tony sent me over. Said if you two didn't have a chaperone, you'd embarrass him by fucking in the bathroom or something."

Sam started laughing, knocking hips with Jace. "Tony knows you pretty well, Jace."

"Maybe he knows you."

"Maybe he knows both of you," Kade chimed in. "Want a beer?"

"Sure," they both said and sat down.

"So where's your roommate?" Kade asked in a casual manner.

Sam looked over at Jace and grinned. "He'll be along."

"There you guys are," Liam came over and flopped down beside Kade on the blanket.

"Yeah. I guess we should get up and mingle." Jace nudged Sam. "But it's a lot more fun to just sit here and drink beer."

"I'm socialised out for a few minutes." Liam whistled. "Woo wee, would you get a load of him!"

Everyone's heads whipped around. Sam had to bite his lip from laughing. It was Lark and his clothing reminded him of

Olivia Newton-John in Grease. The only things missing were the red heels and cigarette.

With a pair of extremely low-rise leather pants, black biker boots and a tight shirt short enough to show his bejewelled belly button, Lark looked like a biker's wet dream. Well, in this case, like Kade's wet dream.

Sam swung his gaze to Kade. No way could he miss his reaction.

Yep, Kade's jeans were about to bust open at the zipper. He jumped up and stood between Lark and the rest of the crowd that had begun to gather.

"Don't you think it would be a good idea for you to go home and put some clothes on?" Kade growled.

Sam almost choked when he saw Lark lick his lips and run a hand over his bared midriff. "Why, don't you like the way I look?" Lark purred.

Yes, his nerdy roommate was actually capable of purring. Sam couldn't believe his ears.

Kade answered Lark's purr with another growl. He took a step forward, putting his body in direct contact with all that skin the small man was flashing. "What are you playing at?" Kade asked.

Sam watched as Kade ground his cock against Lark's stomach. Never before was their height difference so noticeable.

"You'd better run home, little boy, I don't think you're ready to play with the big dogs." Kade took a step back and turned around.

Looking at Jace and Sam, Kade motioned towards the house. "I'm gonna see if there's anything to eat." He walked off without looking back.

Sam glanced at Lark in time to see the tears in his friend's eyes. Lark suddenly turned and ran out of the backyard. "Dammit!" Sam screamed.

He started to go after his friend, but Jace stopped him. "Let Lark get himself together before you go after him. If you do it now, it'll only embarrass him more."

Sam looked from the direction Lark had gone and back to Jace.

"I'm sorry. I told you that would happen," Jace said, putting a hand on Sam's knee.

"I'm not gonna let Kade get away with that bullshit." He stood and stormed his way to the house in search of Kade.

He found him leaning against the kitchen counter eating a hot dog and listening to Joe and Alec talk.

"I need to talk to you."

"Look, Sam. I'm sorry about your friend, but I've got nothing else to say."

"Well then you'd better punch me in the face again, because I'm gonna be in yours until you give me a few moments of your precious time." He stared Kade in the eyes, refusing to back down.

Kade's eyes narrowed as he stared down at Sam. "You're nuts. You really feel like taking me on?"

Sam swallowed. "If it'll get me a few minutes, yeah." God, Jace would kill him if he tried to fight Kade again.

Rolling his eyes, Kade motioned towards the living room. "Five minutes, Suicide Sam."

"Geeze, where do you come up with those stupid names?"

"It's a gift," Kade shrugged and sat on the sofa. "So talk."

Sam started to sit, but changed his mind. "I know why you think you can't get involved with Lark."

"And I take it you disagree."

"Have you been to a counsellor? Because I'm pretty sure there are men and women in the world that go on to lead loving, productive lives after contracting HIV."

Kade stood. "All those people aren't me."

He started to walk away, but Sam reached out and touched his arm. "They could be, you know? I can almost promise it wouldn't make a difference to Lark."

Kade stood frozen for several moments before pulling away and walking out of the room.

Hoping he hadn't just lost a friend, Sam went back outside. He spotted Jace beside the barbeque talking to Dr. Pressman. Sam had spoken to Rocco several times, but it had always been either at the dorm or on campus. For some reason Dr. Pressman intimidated the hell out of him. He wasn't sure if it was because Joe was a doctor or because he was so much older.

Sam stood off to the side and waited for Jace to finish. He felt a nudge to his side and looked over to find Rocco. "Hey," he said.

"Why are you back here when it's obvious you want to stand by your man, as the song goes," Rocco joked.

Not willing to admit he was intimidated, Sam tried to play it off. "When I stand back here, I can take in the full view. Stunning, isn't he?"

Rocco looked Joe up and down. "Absolutely, and don't let the age fool you, he's a tiger in bed." Rocco winked at Sam.

"What are you two up to?" Jace asked, beckoning Sam and Rocco over.

"Just a little boy talk," Rocco answered stepping into Joe's embrace.

Sam took Jace's hand, and was pulled to his side. "Did you get Kade sorted out?"

Saying nothing, Sam shook his head. He hated that two people he cared about were needlessly going home alone.

Jace hugged him closer and kissed the top of his head. Jace must've sensed Sam's present mood. "Let's go talk to the man of the hour before taking off."

"Thanks," Sam whispered. He turned to Dr. Pressman and Rocco. "It was nice to see you both."

"You, too," Rocco said.

They found Bear holding court at the side of the house, surrounded by Koby, Max and Michael.

Bear pushed through the group and hoisted Sam into the air with one of his trademark hugs. "There you are. I was beginning to think you weren't going to say goodbye."

Sam beat on Bear's massive shoulders until he set him down. "I'm here aren't I? Besides, it's not like you're going away forever. I expect you'll show up at our summer place in a month wanting to fish."

Bear's eyes lit up. "Ooh, can I? I haven't fished since last summer."

"Sure, come by anytime." Sam looked at Jace and grinned. "On second thought, you'd better call first."

"Promise," Bear held his hand up. "We'll be gone for about three weeks. First we'll visit my folks and then Liam's mom. Football conditioning starts in July. It wouldn't be a good idea for their new Coach to miss it." Bear beamed.

"Those opposing teams aren't going to know what hit them. Jace and I'll come to as many games as we can."

"Thanks."

Jace stepped forward and shook Bear's hand. "Congratulations on the new job. You'll make a heck of a teacher and a hell of a coach."

Bear smiled and preened. "I like to think so."

Laughing, Sam gave his big friend another hug. "We'll catch up when you get back."

With one last wave, they walked across the yard to their stuff. "I'll get the chairs if you want to grab the cooler," Jace said.

Sam looked around the yard. "Do you think we're being bad guests by leaving so soon? He knew he should stay and mingle, but his mind was on Lark. Where had he gone?

"I don't think so, but it's up to you." Jace ran a hand down Sam's back. "We can always leave for awhile and then come back. I have a feeling the party will go on for quite some time."

"I'm just...can we find Lark?" Sam looked over at Kade. Leaning against the corner of the house, talking quietly to Joe, Kade didn't look any better than Lark.

"Sure. We'll leave this stuff here for now." Jace took Sam's hand and led them to the front of the house.

Sam stopped in his tracks. "Lark?"

There was Lark, sitting proudly on the seat of Kade's Harley. Although he definitely showed signs that he'd been crying, he was all smiles. "What can I say? I'm a stubborn sonofabitch."

Sam started to go to him, but Jace held him back.

"Let me talk to him for a minute?" Jace asked. "Since we know Lark's okay, there's no reason to leave the party. Why don't you go get something to eat and I'll be there shortly."

Sam studied Lark. "You sure you're okay?"

"No, but I will be," Lark answered.

Jace watched Sam leave before turning back to Lark. "I'm going to tell you something that could lose me a friend." He took a deep breath. "Kade has HIV. That's the reason he won't get involved with you. You need to understand that it's nothing personal against you. He's made the decision to abstain from sex of any kind. It's the only way he knows for sure that he won't put someone else through what he's going through."

Lark crossed his arms defiantly. "I appreciate you telling me, and to be honest, I already had an idea of what was wrong with him. I mean, it was obviously something big and no-one was talking about it. You don't have secrets like that when someone has cancer or another illness."

"So you understand?"

"No, not at all." Now Lark seemed to be measuring his words very carefully. "Did you know I'm Canadian?"

Jace couldn't quite figure out what that had to do with anything. "No, I didn't."

"Well I am. My parents moved with a group of their friends to Canada in the early eighties. You see, they wanted to grow hemp for oil and clothing, but the United States government wouldn't allow it. Anyway, they went together and bought a large piece of land. We grow a number of crops, hemp only being one of them."

Jace shook his head. "I'm sorry but you've lost me. What does this have to do with Kade?"

"My parents are what you'd call free spirits. Their friends are also their lovers and everyone is okay with that."

Jace was shocked. He'd never known anyone who grew up in an environment like that.

"When I was seventeen, a man came to live with us. He was looking for a purpose." Lark's face grew dreamy. "He was my first, and I loved him deeply."

"So what happened to him?" Jace couldn't resist asking.

"Nothing. He's married now. Still lives in the compound as a matter of fact. The reason I told you about Bo is because he too has HIV. He had it when he came to us. Before accepting him into the fold of our large extended family, we did our research."

Lark stopped and put a hand on Jace's shoulder. "I know how to keep myself safe. I also know that life doesn't have to stop just because you're positive."

Damn. Maybe Lark was just what Kade needed. Making a decision, Jace reached out and hugged the small man. "I'll do anything I can to help."

"Hey, what the hell's going on?" Kade's voice rumbled behind them.

Jace pulled back and gave Lark a wink. "Nothing, just consoling a friend."

He turned to Kade. "I don't suppose you could give Lark a ride home? The way he's dressed he might get arrested for hustling if he tries to walk."

Lark punched him in the shoulder. "Stop. I don't look that bad."

Jace mouthed the word 'Please' to Kade.

Kade stared at him for several seconds. "I'm headed home anyway. I guess I can give him a lift."

"Thanks." Jace waved goodbye and walked towards the backyard.

Before he disappeared around the corner of the house, he turned back. Kade was digging his jacket out of the motorcycles saddle bag. He handed it to Lark and was demanding he put it on.

Jace grinned and continued on his way. Kade was a smart man. In those low-rise pants, half of Lark's ass was proudly on display. Chuckling, Jace went to find the only ass he was interested in seeing.

* * * *

Sam ran his hands over Jace's shoulders, touching the marks he'd made. "I didn't hurt you, did I?"

Jace grinned and rolled over on top of him. "Are you kidding? It just keeps getting better and better."

"Yeah, it does." He pulled Jace's head down and kissed him. Wrapping his legs around his man, he thrust up. "Can't get enough."

Jace chuckled. "You'll have to give me a few minutes. I'm not as young as you."

"Okay. Maybe I'll just rub myself off. I've got at least two more in me before the night's over."

"God, you're a nympho. And I love it," Jace added.

"Only with you," He groaned as Jace started moving.

"I want you to give up your room at BK. Come live with me," Jace said, nipping at Sam's neck.

Tilting his head further to the side, Sam dug his heels into Jace's back. "I'd love to. Do you think we'll ever make it to class and work?"

"Mmm, we may have to adjust our schedules a bit." Jace ground down and dug his teeth into Sam's flesh.

"Oh fuck!" Sam yelled as his balls drew up tight. Instead of releasing him, Jace bit harder. Sam jerked as he came, moaning Jace's name over and over.

"We're both going to look like lepers by the end of summer," Sam mumbled, coming down.

"By the end of summer hell, more like by the end of the night," Jace laughed, soothing Sam's neck with his tongue.

"Maybe you should start marking me a little lower. That way I can hide it."

"Hmmm, how low?" Jace started licking his way down Sam's chest.

"I'll let you know when you get there," Sam teased, spreading his legs wide in invitation.

Jace sat up and looked down at Sam's exposed body. "Looks like I have my work cut out for me."

"It's a dirty job, but someone has to do it," Sam joked.

"Not someone, me." Jace twisted Sam's nipple. "Remember that."

"No one else. Ever." Sam moaned.

A BIKER'S VOW

Dedication

Thank you, Theresa, for everything you do to make my life a little easier.

Chapter One

As Kade lay in bed, he touched his lips. The kiss earlier in the day from Lark had stunned him. He'd been surprised to say the least.

After he'd helped Sam bring Lark back from a hypoglycaemic attack, Lark had pressed his lips to Kade's. Whether Lark meant it as an intimate gesture or not, it was the closest Kade had come in years.

What would it feel like to hold Lark in his arms? He'd been attracted to the small, five-foot-three man since he'd first set eyes on him. Usually he was attracted to other Alphas like himself. Tattoos on another man made him hot, and he'd never fucked anyone who wasn't proportional in size to his own six-four frame.

Lark was different, with his small wire-framed glasses perched on the end of his nose and his face always buried in a book. He was about the cutest thing Kade had ever laid eyes on. Just thinking about Lark's tight little body had

Kade's cock hard. He plucked at the small silver hoops in his nipples.

Pushing the covers down, Kade wrapped his long fingers around his cock. He rarely indulged any more. Getting himself off had become old and lonely. Now though, just closing his eyes and thinking about the soft kiss Lark had given him was enough to fuel his lust.

He released his cock and spit into his palm before fisting himself once again. *Oh, yeah, that's it.* He pictured the jewel he'd seen embedded in Lark's belly button. Fuck that was hot. He'd never known a man to wear a jewel there.

Grabbing his balls with his other hand, he applied just enough pressure to receive that bite of pain he enjoyed. The more he thought of Lark, the faster he pumped, drawing his legs up to insert a finger into his puckered hole.

He could easily picture running his tongue across all that smooth hairless skin. Dipping his tongue into that cute little belly button before travelling north to what he was sure were a pair of pierced light brown pebbled nipples.

The first shot of cum landed on his tattooed chest, the stream so hot it was like a brand on his skin. Thumb up over the crown to push once again against the slit, and another spurt landed next to the first. He continued the action until his cock was milked dry.

Closing his eyes, he fought to catch his breath. He hadn't had an orgasm like that in four years, eight months, three weeks and two days. His mind drifted to the day in the doctor's office when he was told he was HIV positive. In some ways, a part of him had died that day.

Trying to shake off the maudlin thoughts, he rose and found a dirty bath towel in his laundry bag and cleaned himself up. Tossing it back when he was dry, Kade stumbled back to bed.

As he tried to sleep his mind kept going back to Lark. What would it have been like if he'd never contracted the stupid virus? Would he still find Lark attractive? Unfortunately the answer, he concluded, was no. He wouldn't have given Lark the time of day. Not because the smaller man wasn't sexy, because god knew Lark was one sexy sonofabitch. Nope, he wouldn't have given a staid bookish sort of person his attention.

The Kade of the past was a wild man who liked hot sweaty sex in public restrooms. He loved the smell of a man, the funkier the better. Back then, he drank hard and fucked even harder. Night after night, one or two partners, whatever and whoever he could get his hands on.

Though he generally tried to practice safe sex, it wasn't a priority when his body was full of alcohol and his balls full of cum.

Kade shook his head. *Yeah, fun times that he'd be paying for, for the rest of his life.*

* * * *

The alarm woke Kade the next morning. When he couldn't find the off button, he yanked the cord out of the wall and threw the clock across the room. After realising what he'd done, he grinned. *Perhaps that was a bit extreme.*

Jace barged into the room, still naked. "What the hell was that?"

Kade pointed towards the clock that had come to rest in the corner. "Sorry."

Eyebrows lifted, Jace shook his head and sat on the bed next to Kade. "Bad night?"

Falling back onto his pillow, Kade threw his arm over his face. "Yeah, something like that."

He received a poke to the ribs from his best friend. "Get up. Sam's making pancakes." Jace stood and pulled the covers off Kade.

"Do you mind?" He asked and quickly covered his cock.

Jace chuckled. "Although I've seen every square inch of your body in detail, I can see you wanting to hide that horrible tattoo. 'Free Rides', seriously? If I were going to let someone that close to my cock, I'd at least have something a little more clever."

"Shut up and go put some damn clothes on. Waving that thing around a celibate man is very dangerous." Kade threw the covers back over his exposed lower half.

Laughing, Jace walked out of the room. "You could get some if you really wanted. Not mine of course, but I know a guy," Jace threw over his shoulder as he went into the master bedroom.

Kade's first thought after Jace left was of Lark. With a groan, he felt himself harden and rolled over. Burying his head under the pillow, he willed his cock to get itself under control. Why couldn't he get that little pixy out of his head?

He knew he could fantasise and dream about Lark all day, but that was as far as it could go. Not only was Lark too innocent for someone like him, but spreading the virus stopped any thoughts of a physical relationship in its tracks.

Kade felt himself slipping back into the depression he'd fought so hard against the past several weeks. Turning back over, he swung his legs over the side of the bed and looked down at his now flaccid cock.

Standing, he made sure the hallway was clear before making his way to the bathroom. Kade made a mental list of things he had to do that day. It was the only way he could keep himself out of the rut of depression.

As he started the shower, he began to count things down. Breakfast, go to work, finish up the installation of the marketing department's new computers, eat lunch with Sam and Jace, think of Lark. Kade stopped with the shampoo bottle in his hand. No, he would not think of Lark today, or the fact there was no future for them.

After rinsing his hair, he turned off the shower and dried off. Wrapping the towel around his waist, Kade quickly made his way back to his bedroom and dressed in his usual uniform of faded jeans and a black sleeveless T. He was damn lucky Tony didn't care what he wore. His nicest pair of jeans still had a hole in them, and he didn't think Tony would care for his collection of tight leather pants.

He smelled pancakes and bacon as he walked towards the kitchen. When he stepped through the doorway, he caught Sam and Jace making out. He cleared his throat and went to the cabinet to get down his medicine. When he didn't find them he looked at Jace. "Did you move my stuff?"

"It's on the table," Sam answered, giving Jace a push towards the table.

Kade looked over and saw the four bottles sitting next to his plate. He took a seat and looked at Sam. "You taking care of me now, Sammy?"

Sam took a drink of milk and shook his head. "Nope, just trying to be helpful, and saying thanks for helping me with Lark."

Kade grinned. "No need for thanks. It was a pretty scary situation. Why don't you call him later and make sure he gets in to see the doctor there on campus?"

Shaking his head, Sam swallowed a bite of pancake. "He takes being checked up on about as well as you do."

Kade laughed. Sam knew him well enough already to know he didn't want to be babied because of his illness. He may

133

lean on Jace when things got bad, but there was a special connection between the two of them. Something he'd never been able to get another lover to understand, Jace would always be his best friend. If he were completely honest with himself, Jace had been the love of his life, too bad he fucked it up. Oh well, another lesson learned the hard way.

* * * *

"Hey, mom," Lark said into the phone.

"How are you, Meadowlark?" her soft floaty voice asked.

"Okay, I guess. I had a drop in blood sugar, but my roommate and another guy were here to help me out."

"You know better than to let yourself get like that. Haven't you been eating properly?"

"Yes and no. I haven't been eating as much lately, but I'm still eating." He fidgeted on the bed. He'd always been upfront with his mom and dad about everything in his life.

"I've lost a little weight," he confessed.

"Oh, Meadowlark. We worked so hard to get you at the weight you were. What's happening to change your eating habits?"

Rolling his eyes, Lark fell back on his bed. "A guy, what else?"

"And what kind of trouble could you have with a guy that would make you lose weight?"

"He likes me. I can tell he does, but he won't let me get close to him. Well, except I surprised him with a kiss after he helped me with my hypoglycaemic attack."

"Is he gay?"

"Yeah, but I think he's sick. According to my roommate, Sam, Kade is celibate. He wasn't always that way, just for the

134

last couple years from what I understand. I think he might be like Bo."

"Hmmm, I see. Well, you already know the risks involved so I won't bother repeating them, is he worth it?"

Lark closed his eyes and pictured Kade. "Yeah. He's so worth it, I don't know if I'll ever bring him home. Thankfully Kade's gay and not bi. First I have to get him out of his depression and into my arms."

"I've no doubt you can do whatever you set your mind to. Just be careful and start taking better care of yourself. If you're not healthy, you won't be a lot of good to your young man."

Lark cleared his throat. "Well, Kade's not exactly young. I think he's probably in his mid to lower thirties."

"Oh," she said. "Then we'll have to really watch your father," she said laughing.

"I told you I didn't think I wanted to bring him home," Lark chuckled.

"I'll talk to you later, son."

"Bye, mom. I love you. Give everyone a kiss for me." He hung up and grinned. He knew his mom would do just that.

Setting the phone back on the desk, he looked at himself in the mirror. *What would it take for you to see me as boyfriend material?* He asked an imaginary Kade.

Chapter Two

Sam was packing when Lark walked into the room. He dropped onto his bed, letting his shopping bags fall to the floor. "So this is it? You're really leaving me?" he asked.

Turning around, Sam came over to sit next to him. "You'll see me all the time. Besides, Jace and I expect you to come out to the cabin this summer. We can sit out on the dock and sunbathe in the nude."

Lark felt himself blush. "I'm not sure that I want you seeing me in the nude anymore."

"Why? We've been roommates for an entire year and I've seen plenty. You know for a little guy..."

Lark held up his hand to stop his friend. He'd heard about the size of his cock for years. "Yeah, I know, big things come in small packages, but that's not why I don't want you to see me."

Biting his lip, he tried to figure out how to tell his friend his newest secret. He pointed to the bags on the floor. "I went shopping."

Sam looked at the sacks. "That's nice."

Shaking his head, Lark pulled open the first sack and withdrew a pair of low-rise black leather pants. "I bought these."

Sam's eyes opened wide. "Oh shit. Are those for Kade?"

Lark eyed the pants. He'd been shocked at how good they felt when he'd tried them on. "No, dillweed, they're for me."

"Duh," Sam chuckled. "I hardly think they're Kade's size. I just meant did you buy them to look good for Kade?"

"Oh. Yeah. Why else would I spend three hundred dollars on a pair of pants?" He glanced at Sam. "I went and had myself waxed, too."

"Fuck. Are you kidding me? That shit hurts."

"Tell me about it. Although it wasn't as bad as I was afraid it would be. I'm sure feeling it though." Lark got up and dug in his drawer for a pair of soft shorts.

"Sorry, man, but I need out of these jeans." He turned his back and dropped his pants and underwear before pulling on the shorts. *Ahhh, much better.*

When he turned back around, Sam had the new pants in his hands. "So when do you plan on wearing these?"

"Bear's party," he answered and pulled a pair of black biker boots out of another sack.

"You're going to the party dressed in this?"

"Yeah. Kade will be there won't he?"

"I would imagine, but so will everyone else."

Lark took the pants out of Sam's hand and hung them up. He couldn't help feeling hurt by the flip way Sam had said it. He knew he would be taking a chance, but he also thought

Kade was worth it. He felt a hand on his shoulder and looked down at his feet.

"I didn't mean that the way it sounded. I just don't want you to get your feelings hurt. Kade still seems pretty adamant about being celibate."

"That's okay. He doesn't have to fuck me to love me." *But I hope he does.*

Sam looked at him for a few more seconds before turning back to his packing. "So how long are you staying here?"

"I'm holding out. I talked to Demitri and he said if there are available rooms this summer, I could rent this one for a month. I have to go home in July, but I'd rather stick around for June."

"Your folks have something special planned that you have to go back for?" Sam asked, zipping his duffle.

"Who knows. There's always something going on at Sunrise."

"Sunrise?"

"Yeah, that's the name of the...compound, commune, village take your pick, they all mean basically the same thing. My folks said since I'm going to get out of harvesting for another year I need to at least come home in July to help out."

Lark shrugged. "Small price to pay for everything they've given me." He didn't tell Sam that usually he loved being at Sunrise in the summer, days spent working in the sun, and evenings spent skinny dipping in the lake.

He couldn't believe he was going to give it up for a month to try and convince Kade to take a chance on him. If everything worked out the way he hoped, it would be worth it, if not, well then he'd go home in July to lick his wounds.

* * * *

138

Two days later, Lark studied himself in the full-length mirror. Did he really have the guts to show up at Bear's party looking like this? He adjusted his cock once again in the tight leather pants, enjoying the feel of his smooth groin as he did.

He'd bought the thinnest white cotton T-shirt he could find and cut the bottom off, like Sam had done to his other shirt. He grinned at his reflection as he ran his fingers over the gold hoops in his nipples. They were perfectly visible in the tight top. Damn he felt like a naughty boy.

Checking his hair to make sure it looked properly mussed, he grabbed a couple of dollars and headed out. As he walked down the steps, he crossed his fingers that Charlie wouldn't be in the living room.

He sent up a quick "thank you" when he stepped outside without running into anyone. The cab he'd called was waiting as expected. "This is it," he whispered to himself as he climbed into the car.

* * * *

Although it was only noon, Kade's day had already been shitty. He didn't feel like going to Bear's party. Hell, he barely knew the guy, but Jace had insisted, and Kade knew he'd hear about it if he didn't at least put in an appearance.

Parking his Harley, Kade retrieved the cooler he'd stowed in the trunk of Jace's car. He nodded to Jace's friends as he walked around the side of the house to the backyard. Couples. Everywhere he looked there was nothing but moon eyes and kissy faces. Yuck.

He spotted Jace and Sam under a nice sized shade tree. On his way over he groaned as the two of them started sucking face. "Break it up," Kade said setting his cooler down before spreading out a blanket.

"Uh, Kade? We chose this particular spot because of its privacy," Jace said, tapping him on the shoulder.

"Yeah, well, Tony sent me over. Said if you two didn't have a chaperone, you'd embarrass him by fucking in the bathroom or something." He grinned. Hell, he hadn't even seen Tony yet, but it sounded good. The last thing Kade wanted was to mingle with a bunch of strangers.

Sam started laughing, knocking hips with Jace. "Tony knows you pretty well, Jace."

"Maybe he knows *you*."

"Maybe he knows both of you," Kade chimed in. "Want a beer?"

"Sure," they both said and sat down.

"So where's your roommate?" Kade asked in a casual manner. Shit. Why had he asked that? Now they were going to think he was hot on Lark or something. Not that he wasn't, but he didn't want them to know that.

Sam looked over at Jace and grinned. "He'll be along."

"There you guys are," Liam came over and flopped down beside him on the blanket.

"Yeah. I guess we should get up and mingle." Jace nudged Sam. "But it's a lot more fun to just sit here and drink beer."

"I'm socialised out for a few minutes." Liam whistled. "Woowee, would you get a load of him!"

Kade looked up and saw Lark standing before him. *Oh my fucking god.* He swallowed the sudden pool of saliva in his mouth. His eyes immediately zeroed in on the sweet cock trapped behind the tiny expanse of black leather.

He moved his gaze up to that sexy as sin belly button to the gold rings pressed tight against Lark's shirt. What the hell was Lark trying to do to him? Kade knew all he had to do was stand up and take the little piece of sex on a stick in front of him. The harder his cock became the madder he got.

Didn't Lark know he was only trying to protect him?

He jumped up and stood between Lark and the rest of the crowd that had begun to gather. Even though he knew he could never have Lark, Kade wasn't about to sit by while everyone else ogled him. He continued to look into eyes the colour of the Mediterranean. For once in his life he was at a loss for words. Somehow he needed to get across to Lark that things between them would never happen.

Damn. He'd never wanted someone more in his life. Trapped on the edge of want but can't have, Kade lashed out in frustration.

"Don't you think it would be a good idea for you to go home and put some clothes on?" Kade growled.

Lark leaned towards him. "Why, don't you like the way I look?" he purred.

Vibrating with need, Kade took a step forward, putting his body in direct contact with Lark's. "What are you playing at?" Kade asked and ground the hard ridge of his cock against Lark's stomach.

Angry that Lark could make him feel out of control, he snapped at the younger man. "You'd better run home, little boy, I don't think you're ready to play with the big dogs." Kade took a step back and turned around.

Looking at Jace and Sam, Kade motioned towards the house. "I'm gonna see if there's anything to eat." He walked off without looking back.

With each step he took, he hated himself a little more. By the time he reached the kitchen he felt the acid burning his stomach lining. Grabbing a hot dog off the platter, Kade leaned against the counter and listened to Alec and Joe.

He had absolutely no idea what they were talking about. His thoughts were on Lark's face as he started to turn away. Kade felt his eyes begin to burn and quickly blinked away any evidence that he was upset.

Kade took another bite just as Sam entered the kitchen. "I need to talk to you," Sam said resting his fists on his hips.

"Look, Sam. I'm sorry about your friend, but I've got nothing else to say." *Please go. Just leave me to my own damn misery.*

"Well then you'd better punch me in the face again, because I'm gonna be in yours until you give me a few moments of your precious time." He stared Kade in the eyes, refusing to back down.

Kade's eyes narrowed as he stared down at Sam. The last time Sam had gotten in Kade's face, the young college student had ended up with a broken nose. "You're nuts. You really feel like taking me on?" he asked, setting the remainder of his lunch on the counter.

"If it'll get me a few minutes, yeah."

Rolling his eyes, Kade motioned towards the living room. "Five minutes, Suicide Sam."

"Geeze, where do you come up with those stupid names?"

"It's a gift," Kade shrugged and sat on the sofa. "So talk."

He watched as Sam started to sit, but evidently changed his mind. "I know why you think you can't get involved with Lark."

"And I take it you disagree." Man, didn't Sam care about his own roommate? Sam had witnessed first-hand what he was like when he slipped into depression.

"Have you been to a counsellor? Because I'm pretty sure there are men and women in the world that go on to lead loving, productive lives after contracting HIV."

Kade stood. Yeah, if only life were that simple. He couldn't blame Sam, he had an idealised view of the world. Kade didn't. He'd gone to hell and had taken up permanent residence.

"All those people aren't me," he said and turned to walk away.

Sam touched his arm. "They could be, you know? I can almost promise it wouldn't make a difference to Lark."

Kade closed his eyes, fighting like hell to keep the want and need at bay. When he regained his composure, he walked out of the living room and through the back door.

Finding another beer and a quiet place to be alone, Kade crouched down in the shade behind the little gardening shed. Without taking his lips from the mouth of the bottle he drained the beer.

His mind kept going back to what Sam had told him. Maybe his HIV status wouldn't make a difference to Lark, but did that mean it was fair to him?

Kade put his hand over his chest as it tightened. What was this feeling? Longing? He knew it wasn't love. How could you love someone you'd never held intimately? He had held Lark though, the day of his attack. It was that memory that haunted him.

Dropping the empty bottle, Kade rubbed his eyes with the heel of his hands. He knew he needed to apologise to Lark. What he'd said was out of line. He'd been sexually frustrated and on edge the past several days, and seeing Lark sexier than he'd ever been had pushed him over the edge.

He picked up his trash and went to find Jace. He spotted Sam with a plate of food under the shade tree. Swallowing his pride, he stepped up to his friend's lover. "I'm taking off. Would you do me a favour and see that my cooler gets home?"

"Sure," Sam grinned.

Kade didn't trust that grin. "Something you want to say?"

"Nope. Have a good one," Sam answered and went back to his hamburger.

Shaking his head, Kade rounded the corner heading towards his Harley when he stopped dead in his tracks. There was Lark, sitting pretty as could be, on the back of his bike with Jace's arms wrapped around him.

Oh hell no. No one was stepping in on his man, not even his best friend. The thought surprised him. *Shit.*

Chapter Three

"Hey, what the hell's going on?" Kade yelled as he walked towards Jace and Lark.

Jace pulled back. "Nothing, just consoling a friend. I don't suppose you could give Lark a ride home? The way he's dressed he might get arrested for hustling if he tries to walk."

Lark punched Jace in the shoulder. "Stop. I don't look that bad."

Jace mouthed the word 'Please'.

Kade stared at him for several seconds. He doubted that Lark would get picked up by the cops, but the idea of his little man getting picked up by someone else had him answering right away. "I'm headed home anyway. I guess I can give him a lift."

"Thanks." Jace waved goodbye and walked towards the backyard.

Kade turned to face the little pixy perched on the back of his Harley. He looked down and made a concerted effort to keep his tongue in his mouth. The way Lark was sitting, his ass was clearly on display to the passing cars.

He dug in his saddlebag and produced a lightweight leather jacket. It would swallow Lark's small frame, but at least he'd be covered. "Put this on. I don't need you flashing the cops if they pull up behind us."

Lark grinned and looked behind himself. "What, you don't like looking at my ass?"

"I didn't say I didn't like looking at it. I just don't want a ticket for it. Now put on the damn coat." He watched as Lark did what he was told before climbing on his bike.

"Have you ever ridden a motorcycle?" Kade asked over his shoulder.

"No, but it can't be much different from riding a bike. I just need to keep my balance, right?"

Kade pointed towards the exhaust pipes. "Those get hot, keep your legs away from them or you'll end up with a nasty burn."

Lark surprised him by wrapping his legs around Kade's waist. "Like this?"

When he was able to speak, he shook his head. "You ride like that and we'll both end up in the ditch. Just put your feet on the pegs."

Lark removed his legs, but not before giving Kade's waist a surprisingly strong squeeze. Once Lark was set, Kade started the FLSTN Softail Harley and yelled over his shoulder, "Hang on."

He pulled out onto the street as Lark wrapped his arms around his upper chest. With the passenger seat set higher in back, Lark's crotch rode against the small of Kade's back. He caught himself before a groan escaped him.

The vibration of the bike against his already interested balls, had Kade aroused almost to the point of pain. Lark's hands released their grip on Kade's chest. Automatically, he reached behind him to secure Lark on the bike.

Lark's hands returned. This time pulling the T-shirt out of his jeans and finding their way against Kade's skin. There was no stopping the deep moan that escaped him as fingertips brushed across his nipples.

At a stoplight, he tried to think. His breathing had picked up to the point he could easily hyperventilate if he didn't get relief soon. Making a split second decision, Kade turned the corner and headed the bike towards Jace's house.

He kept telling himself he wasn't going to do anything with Lark, but they needed to talk. Maybe if he explained his reasons, Lark would stop tempting him into a physical relationship.

Pulling into Jace's driveway, Kade turned off the bike and quickly got off. He faced Lark. "We need to talk."

Lark's eyes were already heavy lidded as he ran one hand down over his obvious erection and the other up under his shirt to play with his own nipples. Kade licked his lips, trying to keep his eyes off Lark's roaming hands.

He gave his head a shake. "Lark! You're killing me here. Get off the damn bike and let's go have a beer."

Taking the leather jacket off, Lark held it out for Kade to take. "Do you want me, Kade?"

"You have no fuckin' idea how much I want you, but I can't." He took the jacket and stuffed it back in the bike's saddlebag.

Without turning back to see if Lark was following, Kade unlocked the house and stepped inside. He needed to put some

distance between them while he got his cock under control. "You want a beer?" he asked over his shoulder on the way to the kitchen.

"Sure," Lark answered shutting the door.

He heard Lark enter the kitchen as he opened the fridge. The cool air was refreshing on his heated skin as he studied the bottles for a few moments before pulling two out. Turning, he handed Lark a beer.

Before he could begin, Lark spoke. "You know, you don't scare me."

Kade twisted the cap off and took a swig. "Oh, pixy. There are so many things you don't know about me."

Lark took a couple of sips and set the bottle down. "I think I know the important things. Most importantly, I know how to keep myself safe."

Shit, someone had told him. "Then you know the safest thing for you to do is to stay as far away from me as you can get."

"That's your way of dealing with the virus, but it's not the only way. I can show you."

"Yeah, and how would you know so much about it?" Kade chuckled, "I'd be surprised if you weren't still a virgin."

Kade regretted the remark as soon as he saw the hurt in Lark's eyes. "Not that there's anything wrong with saving yourself. Oh shit, nothing's coming out right," Kade said dragging a hand through his hair.

"I'm not a virgin. I lost that when I was seventeen to a man with HIV."

Shocked, Kade didn't know what to say. The strange thing was, he felt jealousy rise up in him. *Jealous?*

"Who was this guy?" he asked.

Lark shrugged. "His name is Bo. He lives on the land with my folks and a bunch of other people. We knew when he came that he was positive. As a group we did our research before accepting him with open arms."

"And open legs apparently," Kade bit out. "How many others have there been?" Yeah, he was definitely jealous.

"I could ask you the same thing, but I won't. I don't care how many men you've fucked. All I care about is that you give me the chance to get close to you."

Out of reflex, Kade pulled Lark into his arms and kissed the top of his head. "I can't do that to you, baby. Don't you understand?"

"No, I don't think I do," Lark said, his voice losing the confidence it had exhibited before.

When he felt Lark's arm wrap around him in a hug, Kade's jaws clenched. It had been so long since he'd had someone other than Jace offer him a hug. Five minutes, that's all he asked for, just five measly minutes to feel human again.

He groaned when Lark started kissing his chest. "Don't. Just let me hold you."

"Tell me why you won't love me?" Lark's hands burrowed under Kade's shirt to run across his stomach and back.

"Because holding you like this would never be enough for either one of us." He pulled away and sat in one of the kitchen chairs.

He went over and over in his mind how much to tell Lark. He'd never even told Jace the worst of it. "I have no idea if I've infected anyone. Hell, half the time I didn't even know the name of the guy I was fucking. I did use a condom most of the time, but occasionally without. Usually when I was so fucked up I could barely perform at all."

He stopped and looked across the room at Lark. "A real prince, aren't I? It was a fluke that I was tested at all. I was just coming off of a week-long drunk and wrecked my first Harley. While I was in the emergency room I asked the nurse to run a HIV test because it had been more than a year since I'd bothered."

Kade felt his throat constrict as tears threatened. Without saying a word, Lark sat on his lap and wrapped him up in comfort. Brushing his hair out of his face, Lark placed a kiss on Kade's forehead. "I think I can guess the rest. Celibacy is your penance."

"Something like that," he mumbled. It sounded so simple when Lark said it, but yeah celibacy was his penance.

Lark placed his hand on Kade's jaw. "I think you've already paid for your sins. What you have there isn't going away. Spending the rest of your life alone and miserable isn't going to cure you, or anyone else."

Kade felt himself drifting. He'd believed so strongly for years that the only way to live with himself was to suffer. Trying to play off the depths of his emotions, Kade narrowed his eyes at Lark. "Are you just saying these things to get into my pants?"

Lark didn't laugh or smile. Instead, he leaned forward and brushed his lips across Kade's. "No, I'm saying these things because I've seen the kind of life a man can lead despite his HIV status. I think you deserve a little piece of that happiness."

Lark fidgeted on Kade's lap. "But getting into your pants wouldn't be bad either."

Before Kade could say anything, Lark spread his arms wide. "I'm right here. I know full well what I'm getting into. We can start slowly and work our way from there if it makes you feel better."

Kade felt like someone was dangling the promise of everlasting life in front of him. He knew he still had a lot of things to think through and talk out with Lark, but damn how he wanted this man. Oddly, he craved the intimacy two people could share more than the actual sex. It wasn't that he didn't feel like ploughing his cock deep in Lark's ass, but for now, this was good, it all felt strangely right.

"Slow?" he finally asked.

Lark's face lit up with a brilliant smile. "Yeah, as long as making out is considered slow," Lark said rimming Kade's lips with his tongue.

He captured Lark's tongue with his lips and sucked it inside his mouth.

With a moan, Kade placed a hand on the back of Lark's head, holding the smaller man in place while he devoured his mouth. This kiss was a lifetime in the making and he intended to take full advantage.

Just as Lark started rubbing against the hard ridge of Kade's jeans, the alarm on Kade's watch sounded. Breaking the kiss Lark jumped up. "Time for your meds. Where do you keep them?"

Kade sat open mouthed. Maybe Lark really did know what he was getting into. The thought that he wouldn't be taking advantage of a naïve college kid, made him want to pump his arms in the air and shout with joy.

With a smile, Lark gave him one last peck on the lips. "What have you got in mind for dinner?"

You, he thought. "I have some leftover chicken that I bought yesterday. I thought I'd steam some broccoli and fix a baked potato.

Interested?"

"Yep, as long as you throw in at least one fruit."

Kade watched as Lark started flitting around the kitchen, digging stuff out of the fridge. He'd been there for less than an hour and was already making himself at home. While it might put some men off, and it certainly would've him a few years earlier, it now made him feel warm all over.

Chapter Four

Doing the dishes, Lark stole a peek at Kade. He almost wanted to pinch himself to make sure he was really still in the same room with the hottest man he'd ever known. Kade handed him another dish to dry and Lark watched as the snake tattoo on Kade's inner arm flexed. It was almost like a living thing.

Without thinking he reached out and ran a finger over the colourful ink. Kade stilled and Lark looked up into his eyes. "It's beautiful," he said and ran his hand over the tattoo again.

"Thanks," Kade replied. "A friend of mine in Houston did it for me about eight or nine years ago."

"Was it your first?" Lark asked, removing his hand to continue drying the salad bowl.

Kade chuckled and shook his head. "Nope, the one on my right shoulder blade was my first."

Lark had only caught a partial glimpse of the tribal tattoo on Kade's right shoulder. He knew the one on the left was the big one that fanned from Kade's shoulder down and then up to twine around his neck. He'd never seen the whole thing, of course, but the ink on his neck was sexy as hell.

"Will you show them to me sometime?" he asked, taking another plate.

Kade tilted his head. "You into tattoos?"

Lark could feel the blush creep from his neck to his cheeks. He gave Kade a short nod, embarrassed to admit he had his own kinks. "How many do you have?" he finally asked. He hoped like hell that someday he'd be allowed to run his tongue over each and every one of them.

Kade seemed to think for a second. "Uh, fourteen, fifteen? It's hard to say because a few of them have been combined into others."

Fourteen? Damn, his tongue would be busy for hours.

Kade let the water out of the sink. "What about you, pixy? You have any ink?"

Lark bit his lip and shook his head. "Metal, but no ink."

Kade ran his knuckle across Lark's belly button piercing. "Sexy."

His head seemed to swell a bit at the compliment. No one had ever thought he was sexy. Nerdy, bookish, yeah, he'd heard all of those names for years, but never sexy. Deciding to push his luck, he reached down and pulled up his shirt showing Kade the rings in his nipples.

A growl escaped Kade as he moved his hand up Lark's chest, to tug on the rings. "Nice," Kade said.

Lark's cock was so hard it was a wonder it hadn't split the leather of his new pants. He moved slightly and ground his cock against Kade's thick muscular leg. His Prince Albert piercing twisted just enough to torture.

"Oooh," he moaned as he thrust his chest towards Kade. Geeze if just rubbing against Kade felt this good he wondered what it would be like to be filled by him. He knew he wasn't supposed to think of Kade fucking him. That had been part of their agreement, but damn…

He shifted a little more. This time when he rubbed his cock against Kade's thigh, he pressed his abdomen against Kade's trapped erection.

"Fuck," Kade groaned.

Lark smiled. He was glad he wasn't the only one suffering. Kade surprised him by picking him up into his arms. Lark's legs automatically wrapped around Kade's narrow waist as his biker walked them over to the kitchen wall.

Pressing Lark's body against the hard surface, Kade ground against him. "Yessss," Lark hissed. He felt his balls draw up as Kade continued to hump him. "Gonna come," he warned.

Kade quickly reached between them and unfastened Lark's pants, pulling his cock free. The feel of Kade's strong hand squeezing his cock and pressing against the thick silver hoop was all it took for him to erupt. He threw his head back connecting with the wall as he felt the heat of his cum land on his stomach.

"Kiss me," he asked, grabbing the back of Kade's head.

With a moan, Kade's mouth closed over his. Lark delighted at the invasion of Kade's tongue as it was thrust into his mouth. Even though he was spent, he knew Kade had yet to come.

As they continued to kiss, Lark moved back and forth, rubbing himself against Kade's cock. He broke the kiss and looked deep into Kade's eyes. "Come for me," he whispered.

"Aaarrhhh," Kade howled as his body stiffened with the force of his climax.

Lark was a little more than pleased with himself. He knew it wasn't sex, but as long as he took baby steps with Kade, they'd get there.

When Kade opened his eyes, he looked at Lark with a mixture of happiness and sorrow. Lark would do anything to wipe away the sadness in Kade's life. He knew he couldn't do anything about the virus, but surely he could teach Kade to live again.

Kade set him on his feet and turned away. "Um, the bathroom's through there if you need to use it. I'll change and take you home."

It felt like he'd been dismissed, but he knew enough not to take it personally. Kade was angry with himself. That much was evident by the clenched fists at his side.

Excusing himself, Lark walked past Kade and went into the restroom. As he found a washcloth and ran it under hot water, he thought about the hill he was about to climb. He knew Kade would try to pull away.

He closed the lid on the toilet and sat down as he scrubbed the drying cum from his stomach. The big question was should he let him? He knew if he tried to pressure Kade further, his biker would just shut down or take off.

Maybe letting Kade take a step was the right thing to do. He could make sure Kade knew he was there if he needed a friend or a lover and leave it at that for a few weeks. Maybe now that Kade had had a taste of living again, he'd become addicted. One could only hope.

* * * *

Kade pulled up in front of BK House and turned off his Harley. He was acting like an ass and he knew it, but his mind had been whirling since the episode in the kitchen.

"Thanks for the ride," Lark said and climbed off. He handed the leather jacket back to Kade.

Lark started to walk towards the dorm, but stopped and came back. He leaned in and gave Kade a tender kiss. "If you decide to live again, call me. I'll be here until July." Lark ran a finger over the tattoo on Kade's neck. "I like this one the best," Lark said with a smile before turning and jogging to the door.

Kade watched him go, biting his tongue the entire time. He wanted more than anything to call him back, but he needed to think and do some more research. When he'd first found out about his HIV status, he'd made the celibacy decision the same day. He'd never bothered to find out how he could still have sex and keep his partner safe. At the time it wasn't an option.

As he started his bike, he looked back at the closed door. He knew he'd never get a chance with a man like Lark again. His little pixy was definitely a one of a kind. But could he keep him safe? If he didn't get clear answers from his research, he'd walk away.

As he roared out of the parking lot, he realised he had a smile on his face. How long had it been since he'd been this happy? Hell, he didn't even know if he could get involved with Lark, but the prospect alone was enough to lift the heavy burden he'd been carrying for the last couple of years.

* * * *

When he walked through the door, Lark was surprised Charlie wasn't in his customary spot in front of the television. He knew he was upset earlier about Jack taking off the way he did. Maybe Charlie was in need of a friend?

He turned and walked down the hall towards Charlie's small apartment. He knocked lightly not wanting to wake the man if he was already asleep. A few seconds later Charlie opened the door.

"Hey," Lark said. It was obvious Charlie was still down by the haggard look on his face. "Want some company?"

Charlie shrugged and walked back to his chair. Taking that as an invitation, Lark shut the door and sat in the opposite chair. Charlie had a baseball game on his little nineteen-inch television and Lark noticed several empty beer bottles sitting around.

"You okay?" he asked.

Charlie gave a grunt and ran his hand over his closely cropped hair. "Just feeling sorry for myself. Tell me how Bear's party went."

Well, it was obvious Charlie didn't feel like talking about his own problems. Maybe just shooting the shit would help, so Lark leaned back in the chair and got comfortable. "It was good. Didn't start out that way, but the afternoon ended on a high note. I think I'm finally getting through to Kade," he proudly said.

"Kade? Don't you think you should stay away from him?" Charlie asked, brows knitting together.

"Because he's sick?" Lark questioned. He wasn't aware that Charlie knew about Kade's HIV status.

"Sick?" Charlie shook his head. "I don't know anything about his health. I was talking about his lifestyle. I've heard Jace and Sam talking about the wild things Kade's done in the past. The two of you just don't seem to fit, I guess."

With his head resting against the back of the chair, Lark thought about the make-out session in the kitchen. Oh, they seemed to fit perfectly in his mind. "Maybe I'm not as different from him as you think."

Charlie's brows shot up. "There something you need to tell me?"

Lark grinned. It was hard to remember that Charlie was blind. Of course Charlie wouldn't know about the leather pants or the piercings.

"I mean, sorry if this offends you, but I know you're a lot smaller than most men. I also know before Kade started coming around all you did was study."

Charlie seemed a little embarrassed by the observation. Lark wanted to put his mind at ease, so he decided to explain a little about himself.

"You're right, I'm small. I was born eleven weeks premature. I was so tiny the doctors didn't give my folks much hope of my survival, but they never gave up on me. Despite the diabetes, I'm relatively healthy now, my body just never quite caught up." There, that explained his size. "Did you know I'm pierced?" he asked.

Charlie nodded. "Jace told me about the belly button thing. Shocked the hell out of me."

Lark grinned. "Nipples and um…cock, too."

Charlie chuckled and scratched his jaw. "I never would've seen that coming."

He couldn't help himself and erupted in laughter at the comment. Charlie grinned and shook his finger at Lark. "No laughing at the blind man."

"I'm not, I swear," Lark said. "It's nice that you can joke about it."

"Well it's nice that you're not offended by my blind jokes." Charlie's face turned into a scowl. "Some people are."

Lark took 'some people' to mean Jack. Wanting to get away from the topic of Jack, Lark continued. "I grew up in a sexually free environment. Even though Kade thinks he's unique in his past sexual appetites, I'm sure I've seen worse."

Charlie shook his head. "It's amazing how much you can learn about a person even if you think you know them."

"That's what life's all about. If you didn't continually learn new things about the people in your life, your relationship with them would become stagnant."

Charlie nodded his head. "A person has to open themselves for that to happen."

He knew, once again, Charlie was referring to Jack. "Yeah, it's a matter of trust I guess. Maybe some people are afraid of being judged for who they really are. It's all a matter of chipping away at those fears with honesty and acceptance."

Charlie grinned. "Are you sure you're only twenty-one?"

"That would depend on which of my lives you're asking about. In this one? Yeah, I'm only twenty-one." He could tell by Charlie's facial expression that he'd thrown him once again. Reincarnation wasn't something he generally talked about with the average person. It was a personal topic, like all religious beliefs.

Deciding to quit before Charlie thought he was a complete nut job, Lark stood. "I'm gonna get some sleep. You take care and holler if you need anything. Even if it's just to watch one of those horrible sci-fi movies you enjoy."

Charlie stood and followed him to the door. "Thanks for stopping by." Charlie put a hand on Lark's shoulder. "It helped. It really did."

"Good. Then my work here is done for the night. Catch up with you in the morning."

Chapter Five

"Hello," Lark said.

"Hi, um, it's Kade."

Lark grinned. He didn't know anyone else with a voice as deep and gruff as Kade's. "Hi."

"I thought maybe I could interest you in some fishing out at Jace's place after I get off work later."

Bouncing on the balls of his feet, Lark did a little happy dance. "Sure, that sounds like fun." Maybe Kade had made his decision. He doubted Kade would have asked him out if he hadn't.

"I'm getting off early. I told Jace we'd catch supper. Does four sound okay?"

"Perfect," Lark answered. His mind was already on what to wear. He wondered if swimming was part of the plan. Should he wear swim trunks? No, it was better to leave them home. That way, he could always tempt Kade a little further by skinny dipping if the mood struck them to jump in.

Kade seemed to hesitate on the other end of the phone for a few moments. "Something wrong?" Lark asked.

"No. I've been doing some research that I'd like to talk to you about."

He couldn't tell by the tone of Kade's voice if the talk was a good or bad thing. "This is about us, right? I mean, the whole safe sex thing?" He felt a little stupid asking. He already knew that's what it was, but he wanted an idea of where Kade's head was at before their date so he didn't do anything stupid.

"Yeah. I found out there are few perfectly safe activities for us to engage in."

Lark's cock went hard immediately. He knew there were quite a few things they could do that were considered reasonably safe, number one being sex with a condom. Woo hoo! He realised that Kade was still on the phone. Lark quickly got himself under control.

"Okay, well, I'll be out front around four. Should I bring anything? I don't have a pole here, does Jace have an extra?"

"Don't worry. I've got everything under control. I'm looking forward to seeing you," Kade said, his voice dipping even lower at the end.

"Me too, bye, Kade." Lark hung up and went immediately to his closet. Maybe he should go shopping? He walked to the desk and withdrew his cheque book. He'd already paid Charlie room and board for the month, so he should be fine.

Slipping the cheque book into his back pocket, he got ready to leave. He wondered briefly if it was this natural for a guy his age to be so excited by the prospect of a date. He

grinned. He imagined anyone faced with an evening with Kade would be excited. Feeling better about himself, he headed towards the mall.

* * * *

After work, Kade went by the house to change into a wife-beater and an old pair of cut-offs. He'd already had Jace take him to the liquor store at lunch to buy a case of beer that was now icing down at the cabin.

He was nervous. Kade couldn't remember a time when he'd been nervous about a date. He'd even given some thought to shaving his goatee. That was huge. That's when he kicked his own ass and told himself to chill.

Lark was sitting on the bench outside the front door when he arrived at the dorm. Mmm mmm mmm, he thought, licking his lips. He swore that man looked sexier every time he saw him. With a pair of low-riding denim shorts on and a red wife-beater, Lark looked good enough to eat.

Kade turned off the Harley and swung his leg over the side. "You look good," he said to Lark.

Lark blushed all pretty-like and looked down at himself. "I actually planned to go shopping for something to wear, but got sidetracked by Charlie."

"Don't buy anything on my account," he said, pulling Lark into his arms. He ran his hands down Lark's lean back to land on his ass. God, Lark had a great ass. "You look good in anything you wear. Just be Lark and I'll be turned on."

Lark grinned, evidently approving of the compliment. "I could say the same for you, although I'm very turned on by all these muscles you have on display." Lark ran his hands up from Kade's forearms to his biceps. "Did you decide it was safe for me to kiss you?" Lark asked, moving closer to Kade's lips.

"Oh, yeah," he said and stuck his tongue out to run across Lark's soft lips. Kade thought Lark should consider himself lucky that he didn't strip him right where he stood.

"Good," Lark whispered. "Now I can give you a proper greeting."

Bringing Lark into the V of his thighs, Kade kissed him. Their mouths opened wider as they frantically tried to make up for lost time. When he felt Lark's hand land on his cock and squeeze him through the denim, Kade pulled back.

"We'd better get going before we get arrested."

Lark looked so sweet when he pulled back. Kade followed him and gave him one more kiss. "Wait until we've got some more privacy."

Nodding, Lark climbed on the back of the Harley. This time when Lark snuggled up to him, he definitely felt his baby's cock pressing against his back. Starting the bike, Kade felt the rumble under his already sensitive balls, and he knew it was going to be a long ride to the lake.

* * * *

Lark couldn't get over the view of the lake from the cabin's wall of windows. He turned to his old roommate. "You're such a lucky duck."

Sam stood beside him with his arms crossed over his chest and nodded. "Can't argue with you there."

Lark's attention was diverted by the view of Kade out the window. He was down by the shore helping Jace stack wood into a fire pit. Kade lifted the logs like they were made of foam.

Sam caught him looking and jabbed him in the ribs. "How's it going with him?"

Lark's first thought was of the kiss they'd shared earlier. "Good. I think he's coming around."

Turning to lean a shoulder on the window frame, Sam's expression went serious. "He has a problem with depression. Did you know that?"

He could tell Sam was just trying to look out for him. It wasn't said in a gossipy fashion, more an informative one. "Can you blame him?" he asked, looking at Sam.

"I don't want him to pull you down with him. He's been pretty good lately, but from what Jace has said, when it's bad, it's really, really bad."

Lark reached out and gave Sam a quick hug. "Thanks for worrying, but I'll deal with it when or if it happens. We have a lot of other things to work out, that'll just be one more."

When he released Sam and looked back out the window, Jace and Kade were both staring at them with scowls on their faces. "Uh oh."

Sam winked at him. "It's good for them. Nothing wrong with a little jealousy. They both know there's nothing going on between the two of us."

All the same, Lark still didn't want to give Kade a reason to back out at the start of their relationship. "I'd better go out and see if Kade's ready to fish."

Chuckling, Sam walked towards the small kitchen. "I'm making a pasta salad to go with the fish the two of you catch. I'll be out later."

He was suddenly aware of the pressure to provide dinner. "I hope pasta salad isn't all we'll be eating. I haven't fished in several years."

"It's like riding a bike," Sam commented.

Lark walked out the back French doors and down the porch towards Kade and Jace. "You ready to fish?" he asked when he got close enough.

"Sure, let me get the tackle box and two poles out of the shed." Kade started to walk past him but stopped and gave him a quick kiss.

Giving him a smile, Lark watched him walk away before turning back to Jace. "So, how many fish do we need to catch?"

Jace's grin embarrassed him even more. "Three or four should do it." He leaned closer. "And if the two of you get too busy to actually fish, I've got some steaks in the fridge."

Although he knew Jace was teasing him, Lark knew he was happy for his friend. He knew Kade had seemed happier lately, evidently Jace had noticed as well. He saw Kade walking towards the dock, laden with poles and the tackle box. Lark gestured towards him. "I'd better go help."

Jace gave him a little wave. "I'll bring Kade's cooler down and then draw the drapes."

Lark's face felt like it was on fire by the time he reached Kade. "Something up?" Kade asked.

He shook his head. "Jace was just giving me a hard time."

Kade dropped the tackle box and was in front of Lark before he could blink. He put a hand on Lark's shoulder. "What did he say to you?"

Lark was momentarily startled. He hadn't witnessed this kind of anger from Kade before. Shit, he realised Kade misunderstood. "No, no, Jace didn't say anything bad, he was just teasing me."

He cupped Kade's cheek. "It's okay, really."

Kade leaned into Lark's touch. "You'll tell me if anyone gives you a hard time about dating me, won't you?"

He couldn't help the smile that spread across his face. "I could say the same thing to you. I'm not exactly your usual type. Hence the use of the leather pants to get your attention."

Grabbing him under the arms, Kade lifted him to eye level. "I like that you're not my usual type. Don't go selling yourself short. You're a sexy fucker and anyone who hasn't seen it is blind."

Lark wrapped his arms around Kade's neck and kissed him. He didn't think anyone had ever said anything so nice. Kade had hit the nail on the head. He'd always been the shrimp, never the love interest. That reminded him of something he wanted to bring up now that they were dating.

"Will you get mad if I ask you a favour?"

Kade set him on his feet and Lark took a couple of steps back so he didn't have to crane his neck. Kade nodded. "Ask."

"I know you're really good at giving people funny nicknames, but can you not call me pixy? It's kind of along the same lines as squirt and shrimp." He looked down at himself. "I've heard enough cracks about my size." Lark looked out over the water. He didn't want to make a big deal of it, but the name hurt.

Their conversation was interrupted when Jace appeared with the cooler of beer. He stopped at the end of the dock. "Did I interrupt?"

"No," Lark was quick to say. He glanced over at Kade wondering why he hadn't said anything. Kade stood with his hands on his hips and his head down.

"I'll, uh, just leave this then," Jace said and carried the cooler over to set it down at Lark's feet.

"Thanks," Lark said as Jace gave him a questioning look. Lark smiled and shrugged his shoulders.

After Jace went back into the house, Lark reached out and touched one of Kade's hands where it still rested on his hip. "Sorry, I didn't mean to make you mad."

Kade finally met Lark's eyes. "You didn't. I'm not very good at this dating thing. Too many years of being selfish, I guess."

Lark couldn't stand the sadness in Kade's voice. Turning, he sat on the cooler and patted his lap. "Come here and have a sit."

Kade looked at him like he was crazy. But then it happened. A smile began as Kade walked towards him. Lark was suddenly worried that the big guy would actually try and sit on his lap. Instead, Kade picked him up and sat on the cooler, depositing Lark in his lap.

"My dad was in the service growing up, and we had to move a lot. I remember moving to a new base when I was a freshman in high school. The first day of class I saw this really hot guy. He looked me up and down."

Kade shook his head and ran his hand over his goatee. "I thought he was...ya know, checking me out. But then, in front of the entire class, he started laughing and called me Lurch. The entire class started cracking up and I was mortified. When I came back to school the next day, I was a changed man. I found that punk who'd made fun of me and beat the shit out of him. Everyone got the point. Never again would I let someone make me feel less about myself because of my size."

Lark finally realised why Kade was so upset. He wanted to jump in and tell Kade it was okay, but he knew his biker needed to finish it on his own.

"I didn't call you pixy to make fun of you. It was my version of a term of endearment."

"I know," Lark stopped him. He leaned in and pressed a kiss to Kade's lips. "I'm sorry that I brought it up, but since I did, can you think of another endearment?"

"Sure," Kade said. "I'm sure something will come to me."

Chapter Six

Stretched out on a blanket with their poles between them, Lark waited for Kade to start 'the talk'. He was anxious to get a good look at Kade's chest, so he decided to take matters into his own hands, by taking off his own shirt.

Looking at Kade, he tossed the shirt to the decking. He was happy to see the heat in Kade's eyes as his biker's gaze zeroed in on his nipple piercings.

"Are you getting hot?" He grinned, knowing Kade would take the comment sexually. That was fine, whatever it took to get that damn shirt off of that wide tattooed chest.

"What do you think?" Kade grinned back and sat up.

Lark gripped the bottom of Kade's tank, and slowly lifted, exposing the many works of art. The first tattoo he spotted was barely visible above the waist of Kade's shorts. Lark decided he could wait a few minutes before exploring that one further.

As he pulled the shirt up he was struck by the vibrant colours first, shades of light blue, green and purple swirling in tendrils down Kade's stomach. He started to lift the shirt higher when Kade's hands on his stopped him.

"I need you to understand I've had these for years," Kade said.

"Okay," Lark replied. He could tell by the look in Kade's eyes that he was worried. Deciding to end the suspense, Lark pulled the shirt up and off, tossing it next to his own. The swirling fingers of colour became even more vivid as they worked their way towards Kade's left pectoral muscle.

Looking at the centre of the image, Lark's breath caught in his throat. A brilliant red heart was encased in ice. He studied the tattoo for several long moments. It wasn't the tattoo as much as the feeling behind it. He wondered if it was the result of his relationship with Jace or a warning to would-be lovers. Biting his lip, he looked up at Kade's face. "Did you have this done after your break-up with Jace?"

"Yeah," Kade answered.

Lark gestured to the swirling colours. "And this? What does it mean?"

"Chaos."

How one word could so easily allow him a glimpse into Kade's mind was amazing. It was something he definitely wanted to talk about, but by the look on Kade's face he thought it would be better to wait. Instead, he leaned forward and placed a kiss on the heart contained in ice.

Kade fell back onto the blanket, taking Lark with him. Lark lay with his head on Kade's chest as he pulled and plucked at the tiny silver hoops running through his nipples.

"Mmm," Kade moaned and pulled Lark up to eye level. "We need to talk."

Lark nodded and kissed him. Yeah, they did need to talk, but they both needed to kiss more. As usual, the kiss started playful with Lark nipping at Kade's lips, but soon turned ravenous. God, he couldn't get enough. He wanted to crawl inside this big man's body and stay forever.

Sliding his leg over Kade's waist, Lark climbed on top. He couldn't seem to stop himself as he began to move back and forth, rubbing his cock against Kade. Pulling out of the kiss, Lark sat up with his ass against Kade's thick erection. Yeah, this was the position he'd been searching for. He longed to ride Kade's cock. Looking down he tried to convey his thoughts without speech.

Groaning, Kade reached out and stilled Lark's hips. "Talk," Kade mumbled.

Lark warred with himself for several seconds. He knew if he began to move again Kade probably wouldn't stop him. On the other hand, he hated to get himself worked up if Kade planned to put strict restrictions on their lovemaking.

Falling back down to Kade's chest, Lark rested his chin on his hands. "Okay, let me have it," he said with a grin.

Kade answered him with a slap to the ass. "Hey," he giggled and rubbed his butt.

"Behave so I can get through this."

"I promise to be good," Lark replied.

Kade gave him a smile. "I guess I need to know that you've really thought about what you're getting into. I know what you told me, but it's pretty serious stuff."

All kidding put aside, Lark nodded. "I'm so serious about this that I've even told my mom. Of course that was before I worked my magic with the leather pants, but she definitely knows about you."

Kade suddenly looked horrified. "Did you tell her..."

"Yep," Lark said cutting him off. "I've told you, Bo is HIV positive."

"Yeah, and they're okay with you risking your life once again?"

"We don't look at it like that. I mean, we're all gonna die. I was taught to laugh and love today in case tomorrow never comes."

Kade shook his head. "That's exactly the attitude that got me in the situation I'm in. The future's important, and it's even more important to safeguard that future by being safe."

Lark was getting frustrated and he could tell by the twin spots of colour on Kade's cheeks he was as well. "I'm not stupid or naïve enough to suck your cock without a condom, Kade. Geeze, give me a little credit, will ya?"

Kade sat up and ran his fingers through his hair. "Dammit, Lark, I told you I wasn't good at this sorta thing."

Taking a calming breath, Lark climbed in Kade's lap. "Can we just agree to buy a huge case of condoms and use them religiously?"

When Kade didn't say anything, Lark leaned in and kissed him. It wasn't a long drawn out kiss. It wasn't even a kiss of passion. It was a promise. An unspoken, heartfelt promise.

Pulling back, Kade ran his fingers through Lark's purposely mussed hair. "I didn't buy a case, but a pretty damn big box."

One of Lark's brows shot up. "Really? Then what are we wasting time for?" He started to close the distance between their mouths, but Kade stopped him.

"I purposely didn't bring any with me. This date is about spending time with friends..." Kade didn't get any further before his pole took off towards the end of the dock. "Catch it!" Kade yelled.

Lark dove towards the pole, trying to reach it before it ended up in the lake. Misjudging his leap, he ended up teetering over the side with the pole still out of his grasp.

Oh fuck the water was cold. Struggling to surface through the frigid depths, he was thankful when a big hand reached down and caught his arm.

Breaking the surface he looked up into Kade's eyes. His teeth were already chattering. "Sorry, lost the pole." Oh god he thought he might just freeze to death before Kade was able to help him out of the lake.

Kade easily lifted him onto the dock and quickly pulled him into his arms. "You okay?"

Lark's body was shivering as Kade walked him over and picked up his discarded shirt. He smiled around his chattering teeth. For a big biker, Kade could be unusually gentle. He proved it by carefully wiping the excess water off Lark's chest and hair.

"Let's get these shorts off," Kade said reaching for the button at Lark's waist.

"Did you set this up on purpose to get me naked? You know all you had to do was ask," Lark said, trying to lighten the mood.

Kade stopped in the process of unzipping Lark's shorts. Lark suddenly worried Kade wouldn't appreciate his humour in the situation. Kade surprised him by grinning. "An unexpected bonus," Kade said and ran his hand down the front of Lark's shorts.

It would've been sexy as hell if Lark wasn't still so damn cold. He was sure his cock had shrivelled and was even now, attempting to crawl back inside the little warmth his body provided.

For several moments, Kade seemed to be lost in a sexual haze as he stroked and played with Lark's Prince Albert piercing. Finally, Lark pointed towards the blanket. "Please?" he asked.

With a grumble, Kade released Lark's cock and pushed his clothes to the dock. He turned around and retrieved the blanket, bringing it back to Lark. "Sorry, there was no excuse for that," Kade continued to grumble at himself.

Wrapping the blanket around Lark, Kade scooped him up into his arms and took off down the dock. Lark rested the side of his face against Kade's warm chest. "Don't apologise. I liked it, a lot, but it'll be even better once I stop shaking."

Kade carried him towards the house and Lark shook his head. "What are you doing? I'm not ready to leave." He felt stupid enough as it was. The last thing he wanted was to end his first real date with Kade like this.

Without answering, Kade tapped on the door with the toe of his shoe. After several seconds, the door opened and Jace stuck just his head out, his body remaining out of view. Lark grinned, sure he knew what had been going on in the house.

"No fish for dinner," Kade informed Jace. "I'm going to start the fire and get Lark warmed up."

"Take a dip did you?" Jace asked him.

"Something like that," Lark answered.

"I'll get the grill started," Jace said as Kade turned to carry Lark down to the fire pit.

The way Kade held him made Lark feel special. There wasn't anything sexual in the hold, it was a caring gesture and Lark knew it.

Reaching the pit, Kade set Lark down on a smooth log and turned to start the fire. Lark reached his hand out of the blanket and ran it over the smooth old wood. He wondered if someone had taken the time to sand it, or if it was years of being out in the elements that gave the wood its soft texture.

With the fire blazing, Kade returned, once again picking Lark up into his arms. Instead of sitting on the log, Kade sat on the grass with his back against the wood.

Lark curled up and pressed his nude body against Kade's exposed skin. With the fire raging, he was quickly thawing out. "This is nice," he mumbled, placing a kiss on Kade's chest.

Readjusting the blanket, Kade slipped his arms inside. He smoothed his knuckles down Lark's chest. "You warming up yet?"

Lark almost laughed. The feel of Kade's hand tickling at his nipple rings was doing more than warming him up. "I'm feeling down right social again," he joked and stretched up for a kiss.

Kade took his mouth in an all out assault, biting and licking at Lark's lips before delving inside. Lark happily opened for Kade's exploring tongue. As the kiss heated, Kade's hold shifted once again.

The hand that had rested on his back, dipped down to the top of Lark's butt, as the other ran down his chest to encircle his cock. Lark moaned into the kiss as Kade ran a finger down the crack of his ass.

"God I want you to fuck me," Lark said breaking the kiss to straddle Kade's lap.

He must have surprised Kade with the statement. Kade gave him a confused look before breaking out into a smile. Lark loved that smile on his biker's face. Kade leaned in again and ran his tongue around Lark's mouth.

Kade continued to slowly stroke Lark's cock as he talked. "I'm gonna have to either shave or stop kissing you. Your face looks like it was rubbed down with sandpaper."

"Don't you dare do either one. I like it, and I can't wait to feel the rasp of your beard as you're sucking me off." He grinned.

"Pretty sure I'm gonna do that, huh?" Kade asked, grinning back.

"Oh yeah," Lark answered and thrust into Kade's hand. "I bet even now your mouth is watering." Lark wasn't conceited about much, but he knew his cock was a thing of beauty.

"Well, you happen to be right," Kade said. "I've been meaning to talk to you about your Prince Albert, though. Can you remove it without the hole closing up? We wouldn't have to worry about it breaking through the rubber that way."

His PA? Lark only mourned the loss of his most private piercing for a few seconds. There were thicker condoms on the market, but if Kade was worrying about taking a chance, he'd ditch the piercing. He knew Kade was right, but that particular one had brought him more sexual satisfaction than any of the others. Of course... "That's okay. I mainly use it to get myself off anyway."

Kade's brows rose. "Well then, we won't need to worry about that anymore. I plan to keep your dick more than occupied."

"My dick would be more than grateful for that," Lark chuckled.

Chapter Seven

Twenty minutes later, Jace hollered from the deck that dinner was ready. Although he knew Kade was starving, Lark was happy right where he was. Lark looked from Jace back to Kade. "I don't suppose my shorts are dry?"

Kade chuckled. "Nope, I doubt it. Guess you'll have to wear the blanket to dinner. But that's just fine by me. I like knowing you're naked, and open to a questing hand now and then."

Instead of letting Lark walk up the slight hill on his own, Kade stood and hefted him back into his arms. He gave Kade a playful slap on the chest followed by a kiss.

"Jace and Sam are gonna think I broke my legs in the fall from the dock."

"I don't give a shit what they think. I like you in my arms and I'm not ready to give that up yet. Believe me, if Jace could carry Sam around as easily as I can with you, he'd do it."

Lark settled in for the ride. He hadn't admitted it to Kade, but he liked being carried by the much stronger man. He liked the feel of Kade's chest against his face as he snuggled against him. He'd go as far as to say he felt cherished.

Reaching the deck, Kade set Lark in one of the comfortable looking chairs and kissed the top of his head. He glanced at Sam who was smiling at him from ear to ear. Lark grinned back at him.

"So I heard you went for a swim," Sam chuckled. "Water's still pretty cold this time of year."

"That's an understatement," Lark laughed. He looked at Jace. "Sorry, I lost one of your poles in the lake. I'll replace it first thing."

Jace shook his head. "Don't worry about it. I only have cheap ones anyway."

Sam started passing food around the table and Lark let the blanket fall to his lap so he could accept the platter of steaks. He heard Kade clear his throat and looked up in time to see his big biker staring at his friend.

Jace's eyes seemed to be glued to Lark's nipple piercings much to the displeasure of Kade. "Jace!" Kade yelled.

Jace looked away from Lark's chest. "Sorry. I just never really took Lark for the nipple-piercing-kind-of-guy."

The first thing Lark thought of was Sam. He didn't want his friend to get his feelings hurt by Jace's obvious excitement. Sam started to chuckle. "You think I need some of those?" Sam asked Jace, playfully plucking at his own nipples through his T-shirt.

"Hell yeah," Jace answered back, reaching over to brush his hand across Sam's chest.

When everyone realised that Kade still hadn't said a word, they all looked towards him at about the same time. Kade's eyes were still narrowed. "I said I was sorry," Jace said, holding up his hands.

Kade gave a loud grunt. "Next time I see you looking where you aren't supposed to, I'll take your eyes out of their sockets. Got me?"

"Damn, when did you become a caveman?" Jace stood and set his napkin on the table. "I'll be right back."

Lark watched Jace disappear into the house. He'd swear the tension could be cut with a knife. Instead of looking around the table, he casually lifted the blanket back up until it was trapped under his arms. It may not be a comfortable way to eat, but better safe than sorry. He didn't think he could handle Kade and Jace getting into an actual fight over something as trivial as a look.

Jace came back to the table carrying a white dress shirt. He held it out to Lark. "I have absolutely no pants that will stay up on your small frame, but this should be long enough to cover all your vital parts." Jace looked over at Kade. "Well, that problem's taken care of. Can we please enjoy our dinner?"

Kade watched while Lark put the shirt on and buttoned it up, before giving Jace what looked like an apologetic nod.

The rest of the meal was filled with small talk and tales of Lark's dip into the ice cold lake. Kade and Jace started laughing over fishing trips from long ago while Sam and Lark listened in earnest.

Once everyone was finished, they decided to clean up and head down to the fire pit which appeared to be still going strong. Lark rose and looked down to make sure no dangling parts were exposed before gathering an armload of dishes and condiments.

He felt Kade's gaze like a caress as he turned to walk into the house. Had they been alone, Lark would've loved to put an extra wiggle in his walk, but knew it wouldn't be appreciated with Jace sitting there.

Lark started loading the dishwasher when Sam came in with the last armful. He knew he needed to say something to his former roommate, but wasn't sure how to begin. "Um, about earlier."

Sam held up his hand. "Don't. Just because we both love Alphas is no reason to try and defend their actions."

"Love? You think I'm already in love with Kade? This is our first date for crying out loud," Lark said. He wondered if his feelings were that transparent. If they were he'd have to adjust his actions around Kade. Nothing drove a man away faster than the words 'I love you'.

Crossing his arms, Sam leaned against the counter. "I know you love him. I knew you did before Bear's party. I didn't say anything because I didn't know how it would go down with Kade and the whole celibacy issue. That is a thing of the past, right?"

Lark poured detergent into the reservoir and turned the dishwasher on. "We've talked. In theory he's no longer celibate, but we haven't consummated anything. Yet." Just the thought of sleeping all night with Kade, had Lark's cock filling. He knew he'd better get back to his blanket before he made an ass out of himself.

"You sure you don't have a dryer?" he asked Sam again.

Glancing down at him, Sam chuckled and shook his head. "Sorry, this place was built for weekends. We've still been going into Jace's house to do laundry."

Sam pointed at the shirt Lark was wearing. Looking down, Lark realised it might be too late not to make a spectacle of himself. Grinning, Sam waived him towards the door. "Just walk behind me until you can get to that blanket or else World War Three is likely to break out. Jace is only human after all." Sam looked back and gave Lark a playful wink.

Following his friend out the French doors, Lark quickly grabbed up the blanket and held it in front of his lap. Kade rose and walked over and put a hand to Lark's lower back, which didn't help his erection any.

"Ready to sit by the fire awhile?" Kade asked.

"Yeah," he said with a smile. He was surprised Kade actually let him walk down the path to their spot by the fire. He knew Kade had to get up for work at seven. He just hoped they would have time to not only relax, but still make it back to Kade's place in time for some fooling around.

"What time is it?" he asked as Kade pulled him down onto his lap.

Kade looked up at the sky for several seconds. "Eight, maybe." Kade looked over at Jace for confirmation.

"Close," Jace said. "Eight-twenty-three."

As if reading Lark's mind, Jace continued. "By the way, Kade, Tony wanted me to tell you that he doesn't have anything for you to do until around noon. The accounting department didn't get all their stuff moved in time."

Kade nodded and pulled Lark closer, quickly spreading the blanket over him. "You'd think number crunchers would have a better grasp of time."

As Kade, Jace and Sam carried on a conversation about work, and people at work, Kade's hands wandered. Lark's cock was leaking pre-cum like crazy as Kade's hidden hand brushed and played with his hole.

Several times, Lark had to swallow a moan while looking like he was just tired. He closed his eyes and rested his cheek on Kade's chest when what he really wanted was to thrust back and bury that tormenting finger of Kade's in his ass.

He'd get Kade for this. Lark grinned. Yeah, he hoped he'd get him. When Kade's finger pushed inside of him, Lark almost jumped off his lap. Kade never broke the thread of the conversation, just continued to pump his thick middle finger in and out of Lark's sensitised body.

Unable to keep his climax at bay for another second, Lark dug his hands into Kade's waist as he came. He was so proud of himself for not singing the 'Hallelujah Chorus' as his cock continued to empty its seed onto his and Kade's stomachs.

He risked a glance up at Kade's face and found his biker looking down into his eyes. "You okay, baby?"

Was he okay? Shit, he couldn't remember a time when he'd come so hard. He wondered if his feelings for Kade had anything to do with it. He'd cared for Bo, in a teenage boy's way, but he'd never been in love with the man.

Lark didn't answer, instead he gave Kade a grin and smeared his cum into the chiselled abdomen under his hands. He felt Kade's chest rumble under his touch. Lark longed to tell Kade how he felt about him, but it was way too early for that. Instead, he used the tail of Jace's unbuttoned shirt to clean them both.

"You about ready to head out?" Kade asked him, placing a kiss on his forehead. The thought of riding on the back of Kade's Harley bare assed naked wasn't half as unappealing as putting his cold wet shorts back on.

"I don't suppose my shorts are dry?" he asked.

With a chuckle, Kade reached over and picked the garment up from the log beside him. He handed them to Lark and bent to whisper in his ear. "They were dry when we came down after dinner, but I wasn't ready for you to put them back on."

Lark acted like he was going to slap his chest, but pinched his nipple instead, giving the ring a little twist. "You're a bad, bad man."

Kade grinned. "That's what I've been trying to warn you about."

Before Lark could deliver a comeback he heard a noise. Looking over his shoulder, he spotted Sam and Jace through the flames of the fire making out. "I don't think we'll be missed."

He stood and stepped into the dry but stiff shorts. Holding out his hand, he helped Kade to his feet.

Kade picked up his shirt and pulled it over his head.

They looked again at the kissing couple. Kade shook his head. "Thanks for dinner," he said putting his hand just inside the back waistband of Lark's shorts.

Jace and Sam mumbled a goodbye before going back to what they'd been doing. As they walked towards Kade's bike, Lark began to wonder if he'd be asked to spend the night. He couldn't believe this was still officially their first date. It felt like he'd known and loved Kade for years. Precisely the reason he couldn't yet share his feelings.

Lark climbed on the back of the Harley. "You taking me to the dorm?" he finally asked as

Kade got on in front of him.

Reaching back, Kade pulled Lark closer. "Don't count on it," Kade said as he started the bike.

They took off down the gravelled road back to town. Lark's stomach did flip flops at the thought of being filled by Kade. That reminded him. He'd already come once but he'd left Kade high and dry. What kind of lover must Kade think he was?

Running his hands down Kade's chest, Lark covered the erection between his biker's spread thighs. Kade's body jerked just enough to let Lark know he approved. Unfastening Kade's shorts, Lark couldn't wait to get his hands on Kade's cock. His fingers travelled through the thick nest of hair before going deeper. The thick veins running up

Kade's length stood out in stark contrast to the otherwise smooth skin.

Shit, he had to see Kade come. Without thinking he leaned around Kade's wide body. What happened next went by in a blur. His leg lost its grip on the seat as he started to fall. Realising what was happening, Kade must've released one hand from the handlebars to try and catch him.

Lark wasn't sure if they hit something in the road or if it was the unbalancing of the bike, but he suddenly saw the gravelled road rushing up to greet him. He heard the crunch of metal as the Harley fell to its side, as he rolled, trying like hell to protect his face. He came to a stop in time to see Kade land in a ditch about ten yards away.

Oh fuck, what have I done?

Chapter Eight

Lark managed to get his feet under him as he made his way across the road towards his fallen man. "Kade," he called as he scrambled down the ditch's incline. Kade was rolled into a foetal position on his side, holding his leg. All he could think about was Kade's safety. How would he live with himself if his biker was seriously injured?

He knelt and put his hand on Kade's shoulder. Kade jerked his head around and pulled back. "Don't touch me!" Kade yelled.

Lark reared back. "I'm so sorry," he said, already feeling the tears dripping down his cheeks. He hadn't meant to do something so stupid and reckless. He knew Kade was angry with him, but he also knew the man needed help.

"Come on, let me help you," he said, reaching for Kade once more.

What happened next surprised him more than the wreck itself. Kade reached out and slammed Lark in the chest with the palm of his hand. "Goddamit, I said stay away from me."

Lark fell back like a rag doll, his head landing hard on the ground. For several seconds he saw stars and was afraid he'd pass out. He wondered if Kade had cracked his rib. He was heartbroken. One hand went to his chest and the other covered his face to hide his anguish. One careless act and any chance he had with Kade was apparently over. Had it only been twenty minutes since he'd come in Kade's arms?

Getting his emotions under control, Lark knew he still had to do something to help Kade. He may get knocked on his ass again, but he couldn't sit and do nothing. He heard Kade moaning in pain. "Where's your phone?" Lark asked as he stood over Kade.

He braced himself for another blow. "Kade? Where's your phone?"

Kade said nothing but pointed towards the bike.

"Shit," Lark said as he made his way to the wrecked Harley. The once beautiful grey and black paint job appeared perfectly intact on the side that was face up. Lark knew the other side of the bike hadn't fared as well. The chrome handlebars were twisted, as the back tire continued to spin.

The first thing Lark did was turn off the engine. He wasted precious seconds waiting for the rear tire to stop turning so he could safely get to the saddle bags. The momentary lapse in activity drew his attention to his own cuts and scrapes. He looked down at Jace's shirt and was surprised to find it dotted with spots of blood and several holes. Reaching up to wipe his brow, he winced. What he took as sweat dripping from his forehead, was in fact blood.

Kade's moans brought him back to the task at hand. He dug through the bag on the back of the bike and found nothing but the leather jacket. He kept it out and walked around to the other side of the bike. Unable to get to the other saddlebag, Lark knew he was going to have to turn the bike over.

Using every bit of strength he possessed, Lark tried to lift the seven hundred pound bike. When it barely budged, he looked back at Kade.

Stretched out in the grass, Kade appeared to be either passed out or...

"Kade," he yelled running back down into the ditch.

Kade opened his eyes. "Did you get the phone?"

Lark shook his head. "I can't lift the bike. I'm gonna have to run back to Jace's." He couldn't tell if Kade was still angry with him, but he wanted so much to comfort him.

"What's hurt?" Lark asked.

Kade turned over and Lark was able to see Kade's injured leg for the first time. He covered his mouth as he knelt beside his lover. Kade's thigh had been pierced clear through by a survey marker during the fall. "It's bad," Kade mumbled.

"Here," he said handing Kade the leather jacket as he noticed the big body shivering visibly. "Will you be okay if I run back to the cabin?"

Kade nodded. Lark stood and started to turn towards the road. "Lark," Kade said softly.

Lark turned back to his lover.

"I'm sorry I pushed you." Kade shook his head. "I just couldn't take the chance of infecting you."

So that's why? Lark fell to his knees once more. Careful not to touch his downed biker, Lark leaned a few inches from Kade's face. "I love you. If it meant saving your life, your blood would be the least of my worries."

He didn't tell Kade that he was afraid one of his ribs had been injured in the incident. Kade's eyes were boring into his. "Does that freak you out? That I love you, I mean?"

"Yeah, a little. It freaks me out even more to know I'm falling pretty heavily myself," Kade mumbled. Lark noticed his speech was getting harder and harder to understand.

"Did you cut the inside of your mouth?" Lark asked.

Kade's brows furrowed. "No. Why?"

Lark covered Kade's lips with his own. He thrust his tongue inside. Drawing back, Lark looked down at Kade. "Hang in there. I'll be back as soon as I can."

He stood and started running back down the road as fast as his sore ribs would let him.

* * * *

By the time he reached Jace's cabin, Lark was in real danger of passing out. His vision had begun to dance almost a half-mile down the road. For someone as out of shape as he was, it was a wonder he'd been able to run the full four miles or so.

As he ran into the yard, Lark used what was left of his energy to call for Jace and Sam. Falling to his knees, Lark prayed they'd get back to Kade in time.

Lark heard feet slapping against the dry earth and looked up. "Shit, Lark, what happened?" Jace said trying to pull Lark to his feet.

"Wreck, Kade's hurt," he panted.

"Get the keys," Jace yelled back to Sam who was rounding the back of the house.

Sam disappeared inside before darting back out, phone in one hand, keys in the other. He tossed the keys to Jace and wrapped an arm around Lark. "What happened?"

As they loaded him into the car, Lark told them everything. How he'd caused the accident. How he was unable to lift the bike to get to the phone, about Kade's injury. The only thing he left out was Kade's anger. He didn't want to think about that, and he didn't want to see the pity in his friends' eyes when he told them.

Sam called for an ambulance as Jace sped to the accident scene. When he slammed on the brakes, Lark grabbed his chest and groaned in pain.

Jace opened the door and looked in the backseat. "You hurt?"

Lark shook his head. His stupid ribs weren't as important as helping Kade. Schooling his features, he got out of the car and went to Kade. He wasn't surprised to see Kade's eyes closed. As much pain as his lover had been in earlier, it was probably better this way. Squatting at his lover's side once again, Lark checked Kade's pulse as Jace looked at the leg injury.

When Jace made no move to actually do anything, Lark snapped. "He's gonna bleed to death." Lark quickly took off his white dress shirt and started wrapping it around Kade's bleeding leg. "Why the fuck are you just standing there?" he cried.

Jace reached down and tried to pull Lark away. "Lark! Don't touch him."

Lark snapped his head around to stare at Jace. "What the fuck, he's your friend. Are you really going to stand by and let him die?"

"His blood..." Jace started to say, but Lark cut him off.

He pulled away and went back to applying pressure to Kade's leg. "I don't give a flying fuck what Kade's got. The man I love could be bleeding to death. That's what I care about. If you're not going to help, get the fuck out of here."

Lark heard Sam say his name, but he didn't bother to turn around. He could hear sirens in the distance. Once he knew help was on the way, Lark lost it. Stretching out, he kissed

Kade's slack lips. "Please don't die because of me," he whispered. "I don't care if you never speak to me again as long as you live. Come on, sweetheart. Open your eyes for me."

He heard Jace shouting to the medics, moments before they appeared at Kade's side. "You'll have to move back, sir," one of the guys said.

This time, when Sam and Jace appeared, he let them lead him towards the road. He paced back and forth beside the ambulance as he watched the paramedics start an IV and get Kade loaded on a narrow gurney. He heard Kade mumbling and felt a little better. At least his man was conscious.

"Lark you need to get your hands cleaned," Jace said.

He looked down at himself. It was hard to tell where Kade's blood began and his ended. "I'll be careful until I get to the hospital." He made a mental note not to touch anything, including himself.

Sam ran to Jace's car and came back with a pair of leather gloves. "Put these on until we can get you cleaned up."

Nodding, he took the gloves, being careful not to touch Sam as he put them on. The medics carried Kade out of the ditch and to the waiting ambulance. Lark couldn't help notice the plastic face shields and thick latex gloves they wore. *Of course. They don't love him like I do.*

"Come on," Jace said to him as they loaded Kade. "We'll follow them into town."

As they shut the doors, Lark looked through the small square windows. His breath caught as he made eye contact with Kade. He couldn't read his lover's facial expression. Was Kade still mad?

The ambulance pulled away and Jace hollered at him to get in. Climbing into the backseat, he sent a prayer of thanks out to the universe, Kade was still alive.

* * * *

Stepping into the bright lights of the emergency department, Lark immediately went to the desk. They'd gotten separated from the ambulance as they drove into town and he needed to know Kade's condition.

"The ambulance just brought in a man, Kade Straus? Can you tell me if he's going to be okay?"

The woman looked up from her computer screen. Lark couldn't help but notice her wide-eyed stare. "Were you in the same accident?"

"Yes, ma'am," he answered.

She picked up the phone and within seconds, a nurse was standing beside him. "What? Is it Kade?" No, no, no, he was looking into his eyes just ten minutes earlier. Lark turned around to look at Jace and Sam.

"Go with the nurse and let her clean you up and check you out," Jace said.

"But Kade?" he questioned. What was wrong with these people? "I'm not going anywhere until I find out about the man I love." Pissed, he turned to the nurse. "Get me some information and I'll go with you."

Crossing her arms, the middle-aged nurse looked him up and down. "Come with me and I'll find out how your…boyfriend is."

Lark knew the longer they stood arguing, the longer it would take him to find out what he wanted. "Fine," he said and let the nurse lead him through the automatic doors.

* * * *

As soon as Lark was shown to the small exam room, the nurse disappeared to find out about Kade. After asking him to remove his soiled clothes, the nurse, Lynetta, her nametag proclaimed, donned protective gloves and a surgical gown. As Lynetta cleaned the tainted blood from his arms, chest and face, Lark couldn't help but to feel ashamed of himself. It was a totally new experience having someone leery of touching him. Was this what Kade felt everyday?

He'd learned that they'd taken Kade to surgery to remove the wooden stake from his thigh. According to Lynetta, removing the piece of wood would no doubt increase the bleeding. In the operating room, they could quickly seal the wound.

"We'll need to get that head stitched up and some x-rays on your chest," Lynetta said.

"X-rays? I know my chest is a little sore, but I doubt it's anything serious." He looked down at his chest for the first time as she wiped away the blood. *Oh fuck.* There was almost a perfect handprint bruised into the area of his right rib cage where Kade had pushed him. Is that why Sam had gasped? Did they know Kade had done it?

Lark looked back up at Lynetta. He didn't know why he felt the need to explain the bruise to her, but he did. "My boyfriend didn't want me to touch him. When I insisted, he pushed me away."

One of Lynetta's brows rose. "I normally would never condone such a thing, but given the circumstances, I think he did it because he cared about your safety."

"What will happen to me? I mean, do I get tested, or what?"

"You'll need to discuss this with the doctor, but I would imagine he'll start you on *Post-exposure prophylaxis* which is a fancy name for PEP."

"How does that work?" Lark asked, as she finished cleaning him up.

"Well, you'll probably be started on three different antiretroviral medications right away. They're usually taken for four weeks." Lynetta set the basin of bloody water aside. "From what I understand, the side-effects aren't pleasant."

Lynetta helped Lark off the table. "You'll most likely experience some nausea, headaches, fatigue and possibly vomiting. Are you out of school for the summer?"

"Yes, ma'am," Lark answered automatically. How would he be able to take care of Kade if he wasn't feeling well? Lark knew he didn't want Kade to know he'd come into contact with Kade's blood after he'd passed out. Hopefully he could convince Jace and Sam to keep his secret. Kade would never forgive himself if he knew.

After dressing in an open backed hospital gown, a young resident came in to stitch his forehead. Lark was so busy working out details that he barely noticed.

Once the x-rays were taken and it was determined that his ribs were merely bruised, Lark had a long talk with a doctor. He was given prescriptions for the PEP medications he'd need to take for the next four weeks. Then he was released.

Chapter Nine

Walking out to the waiting room, Lark was greeted by not only Jace and Sam, but Charlie as well. After receiving hugs from his friends, Charlie passed him a small duffle bag.

"I thought you might need some clothes," Charlie said. "I don't know if they match, but they're clean."

"Thanks," Lark said. He pointed towards the restroom. "I'll go change."

As he went into the over-sized handicapped stall, Lark still felt a little numb. He knew he needed to talk to Sam and Jace about what had happened earlier at the accident scene. Well, first he needed to apologise and then he needed to beg them to keep his secret.

After dressing, he went to the sink and looked at himself in the mirror. The small bandage on his forehead was the only injury visible with the long sleeved shirt Charlie had packed.

He made a mental note to call home as soon as he knew Kade was out of danger. He was tempted to run to the nearest pay phone and do it right then, but Lark knew he needed to pull on his big boy pants, and handle this without his mom's help.

Picking up the empty bag and hospital gown, Lark stepped out of the restroom. He dropped the gown off at the nurses' desk and rejoined his friends. "Any word?" he asked.

Jace nodded and drew Lark over to a group of seats in the corner. "The doctor came down while you were getting changed. He said Kade was out of surgery and doing fine. He lost quite a bit of blood, and they had to repair a torn muscle, but he said Kade would be fine after a couple of physical therapy sessions. We can go up in about an hour."

Lark exhaled the breath he hadn't realised he'd been holding. Okay, everything was going to be okay. They could do this. He could help Kade with his physical therapy and they could continue where they'd left off. Shit, that reminded him.

"I don't want Kade to know about his blood getting on me," Lark said, looking at the three shocked faces of his friends. "We all know he'll blame himself."

Jace shook his head. "I can't lie to him, and you shouldn't either." Jace looked at Sam. "A simple lie almost broke me and Sam up. This is a lot more than simple."

Lark's thumb automatically went into his mouth to chew the already short nail. Sure Jace was right, but he knew Kade would pull away from him when he found out he'd been exposed. Should he tell Kade right away, or wait until he asked?

"I need to find a pay phone and call my mom," Lark said, looking around the waiting room.

Sam held out his cell. "Here, take mine. It'll give you more privacy."

Thankful, Lark took the phone. "Thanks. I'll call collect."

"Don't worry about it," Sam said with a squeeze to Lark's shoulder.

Nodding, Lark walked out to the parking lot. He found a bench and dialled home.

"Hello?" his father answered.

"Sorry to wake you, Dad," Lark replied, picking at his thumb nail again. "Can I talk to Mom?"

He heard sheets rustling in the background and more than two voices exchanging conversation. *Typical.*

"Meadowlark? Is something wrong?" his mom asked when she finally got on the phone.

Just the sound of her soft melodious voice had tears stinging Lark's eyes. "Kade and I were in a motorcycle accident."

"Oh, baby, are you okay?"

He heard her tell his dad and whoever else was in the room. "I'm fine," Lark said. "I have a couple of bruised ribs, road rash and a couple of stitches in my forehead. Kade didn't fare so well, he landed on a wooden land surveyor's stake. He just got out of surgery, but he should be fine."

"Oh, thank the heavens," his mom replied.

He knew he needed to tell her all of it. Lynda Wilsher was the most level headed person he knew. If there was real reason to panic, he'd know soon enough.

"I was exposed, Mom. Kade was bleeding, and I couldn't sit and not help him." He was glad he'd already warned his mom about Kade's HIV status.

"Of course you couldn't. What does the doctor say?"

"He's got me on a round of meds. He said I'll probably suffer from side effects, but they're my best hope."

"Come home," his mother said. "There are plenty of people here who can help take care of both of you."

Lark heard conversation in the background. He knew home was the best place for him and Kade. They had the facilities to help his lover with his physical therapy. Home also had Bo, who would be a good example for Kade. He hated to bring it up, but he needed to make a couple of things clear before he dared take Kade to Sunrise Gardens.

"Will you make sure everyone there knows that we aren't into the lifestyle?"

There was a pause. Lark started to worry that he'd offended his mom. "You're in love," she finally whispered.

"Yeah," he admitted. "And I won't take the chance of losing him to anyone there."

"We'll respect your wishes," she said.

"Thanks."

"So, when can we pick you up at the airport?"

"I don't think Kade likes to fly. We'll probably drive up as soon as he's up to it."

"Do you need me to wire you some money for a car?" she asked.

Lark grinned. "Not yet. I still need to talk to Kade. If he doesn't want to go, I'll be staying here. I'll call you later, though, to give you a definite answer."

He heard her talking to the others in the room. After a few grumbled replies, he couldn't help but to ask. "Mom? Who else is there with you besides dad?"

There was once again a long pause. "His name is Neil Bancroft. He's new to the farm since you left. Uh, we'll have to discuss it when you get here."

Lark was taken aback. This behaviour was not like his normally open mother. "Mom? Is something wrong?"

"No, not wrong at all. It's just something I'd rather tell you in person. Don't worry, Meadowlark, it's a good thing."

His mind was reeling. As much as he wanted to question her further, he knew she wouldn't budge on the topic. "I love you," he finally said. "I'll let you know what our plans are when we figure them out."

He hung up the phone and just sat there. Well, at least she didn't seem overly concerned about him contracting Kade's virus. Maybe the calm atmosphere of the farm was just what Kade needed to prove he could lead a long and productive life.

* * * *

A hand to the back of his head woke Lark several hours later. He blinked several times and wiped the drool from the corner of his mouth. When he could focus, he realised his head was lying on a mattress while the rest of him was in a very uncomfortable chair. *Kade!* He thought, lifting his head.

Kade smiled at him. "Hey, sleepy head."

Lark jumped out of his chair and leaned over to kiss his man. With his bruised ribs, the movement hurt like hell, but he schooled his face. "I'm so sorry," he said, breaking the kiss. He looked down at Kade's leg. "How're you feeling?"

"Okay. Tired." Kade's eyes went to the bandage on Lark's forehead. "What about you?"

"I'm fine." There was so much Lark wanted to say, but he could tell by the glazed look in Kade's eyes that he was still under the influence of pain medication. He ran his fingers through Kade's long black hair, trying to work out several knots.

"I'll go down to the gift shop and buy a brush," he finally said.

Kade grinned. "Do I look that bad?"

Lark shook his head. "You could never look bad to me."

He closed the distance and placed another soft kiss to Kade's lips. Kade moaned and opened his mouth, teasing Lark's lips with his tongue. Lark immediately opened and closed his eyes as Kade's tongue invaded his mouth. Yeah, kisses were good. He knew once Kade found out about the exposure, he'd try to pull away.

The kiss grew in intensity and before long, Kade was trying to tug Lark down on top of him. Giggling, Lark broke the kiss and shook his head. "As much as I'd love to climb on top of you, I don't think your leg or the nurses would appreciate it."

"Fuck 'em," Kade growled. "I could've lost you," Kade said soberly.

Lark knew just how Kade felt. He'd thought of the same thing while waiting for Kade to wake up.

Kade tried pulling him down once more. "Please," his big biker begged.

Lark stood and studied Kade for several seconds. With a dramatic sigh, he went around to the other side of the bed away from Kade's injured leg. "Can you scoot over any more?"

"If I did that, you wouldn't be close enough," Kade joked.

Now it was Lark's turn to smile. Kade definitely felt good if he was able to tease. Of course the doctor had told them Kade would be fine, Lark just refused to believe it until he saw it with his own eyes.

With his hands on his hips, he looked at Kade. "Fine," Kade said and scooted over a couple of inches. Deciding to leave the guard rail in place, Lark crawled up from the end of the bed to Kade's side.

"Are we taking a nap?" he asked as he tucked himself against Kade's chest.

"Sounds like a good idea, baby," Kade responded, pulling Lark closer.

Within minutes they were both asleep.

* * * *

Two days later Kade sat on the side of his bed waiting to be released. Lark was once again in the restroom and Kade was starting to worry. His little man had been looking a little green around the gills lately although he continued to insist he was fine.

A sound at the door had him lifting his head. "Come in," he called.

Jace and Sam stepped inside. "Ready to go home?" Jace asked.

"Yep, as soon as I can get signed out," Kade answered.

"Where's Lark?" Sam asked.

Kade pointed towards the restroom door. "I don't think he's feeling well." He saw the looks Sam and Jace passed between them. "Is there something I should know?"

Sam's eyes rounded and Jace tried to change the subject. "So have you decided to go to Canada for the rest of the summer?"

"Yeah, but answer my question," Kade demanded.

"They have me on PEP meds," Lark confessed, stepping out of the restroom, wiping his mouth.

The news hit him like a ton of bricks. "What?"

"It's just a precaution. With the amount of blood at the scene of the accident, the doctor thought it was a good idea." Lark walked over and stood in between Kade's legs. "I didn't want to tell you because I knew it would only get you upset."

Kade wasn't sure how he felt. He looked into Lark's eyes and placed his hands on his lover's slim hips. "You touched me, didn't you?"

After a few seconds, Lark closed his eyes and nodded, crushing himself against Kade's chest. "I was so afraid. There was so much blood, and I couldn't take the chance of you dying without doing something."

Lark pulled back enough to look Kade in the face. "I'd do it again. I love you."

Kade knew it would take a while for what had happened to sink in, but in the meantime, the words Lark had uttered filled him with joy. Someone loved him enough to risk their life. Had he ever really had that? He knew at one time Jace had loved him, but sadly, Kade had never really felt it, until recently.

"How long will these side effects last?" he questioned Lark.

"I'm not sure. I'm on the medication for four weeks. That's why mom wants me to come home."

Kade was shocked. "She knows?" How in the hell did Lark expect him to face an outraged mother?

"Yeah. I called her after I knew you were gonna be okay."

Lark seemed to read Kade's mind and cupped his cheeks. "She's not mad. You'll never meet a more understanding woman. I told her I wouldn't come if you weren't with me." Lark placed a kiss to Kade's lips. "She knows how much I love you and embraces it."

Kade pulled Lark's head back to his chest. He was torn. The last thing he felt like doing was getting on a plane, but with Lark feeling sick all the time, how would he endure a two, or three-day car ride?

He still wasn't sure how he felt about going to Canada, but he knew Lark wanted to go home. The old Kade would've just driven him to the airport, but he wasn't the old Kade anymore. Now he had someone worth fighting and living for.

"I guess we need to book a couple of airline tickets," he said looking over the top of Lark's head to Jace. "Do you think Tony will be upset if I quit without notice?"

Jace shook his head. "Not as long as you call him if you ever need your job back."

Chapter Ten

Sitting on the floor of Kade's bedroom, Lark was brought out of his trance-like state, by a grumble from the bed. "What the hell are you doing on the floor?" Kade's sleepy voice asked.

Lark looked over his shoulder and smiled. "Meditating. I usually do it at least once a day. I'm hoping it'll help settle my stomach."

Kade shook his head and lifted the sheet, exposing his beautiful naked body to Lark's view. "Well if you're done, drop your drawers and get in here."

Lark untangled his legs and stood. Kade had fallen asleep as soon as Jace and Sam had helped him into bed. Lark usually did his meditation nude, but kept his boxer-briefs and T-shirt on this time. The last thing he wanted was for Kade to see the purple and blue bruise on his chest.

Walking over to the bed, Lark sat on the edge and stripped out of his underwear. Crawling under the covers, he pressed himself against Kade's warmth. "That better?" he asked, running his hand down Kade's chiselled chest and abdomen.

Kade let the sheet fall and started tugging on Lark's shirt. "Almost, but we need to get rid of this."

Taking a deep breath, Lark removed his shirt without exposing himself. A round of nausea hit him as he flung the garment to the floor. Sweat immediately popped out on his forehead. He closed his eyes and swallowed several times, willing himself not to throw up.

"You okay, baby?" Kade asked, wiping the perspiration from Lark's face.

Lark managed to give his head a little shake. "Just need a second." The side effects of the medication seemed to get worse all the time. No wonder a lot of people quit taking them before the full four weeks were up.

Knowing he was losing the battle, Lark sprang out of bed and quickly raced out the door towards the hall bathroom. As he knelt in front of the toilet, he retched violently, losing what little food he was able to eat for dinner.

He heard arguing in the hallway outside the door, but he was too sick to worry about what else was going on in the house. Lark heard the door open as he retched again.

"Goddamit, just help me get to him then, you old mother hen," Kade was yelling at Jace.

"You're gonna start bleeding if you don't take it easy," Jace replied.

A cold cloth was pressed to his forehead as Kade's deep voice began to soothe him. He felt Jace brush his bare back as he helped Kade to the floor.

"It'll be okay," Kade said.

Even though his stomach was now empty, Lark continued to heave. He began uttering the same nonsense most people did in the same position. "Oh god, I just want to die," he said several times in quick succession.

"Shhh," Kade said, wiping Lark's forehead again. "Don't say things like that. We'll get through this."

Lark rested his forearm and head on the toilet seat, feeling totally wrung out. Kade pulled him back into his lap and Lark settled against his lover's chest.

"Maybe we should call the doctor. Surely most people don't have side effects this severe," Kade said running his hand down Lark's back.

Lark shook his head. "I'll be fine. I just need to rest for a little while."

"Jace!" Kade yelled.

Lark heard two sets of footsteps in the hall moments before the door opened once again. "Help me get him to bed, will ya?" Kade asked.

He was so tired he didn't even have the strength to feel embarrassed as Jace plucked his naked body from Kade's equally nude lap. Lark rested his head on Jace's chest and closed his eyes. He heard Sam helping Kade up from the floor as he was carried from the bathroom back to Kade's bed.

"Thank you," he mumbled as Jace placed him on the cool sheets.

He opened his eyes to look at the concern in Jace's face. "I know you don't feel like it, but you need to drink something. The last thing I'm sure you want is to wind up in the hospital suffering from dehydration," Jace said as Sam helped Kade into the room.

"Yeah," Lark said. "Just some water."

"How about a sports drink?" Sam asked. "I think we have some in the fridge."

Lark shook his head, fighting to keep his eyes open. "Can't. Diabetic."

"Shit," Sam said. "I completely forgot about that. Should we be doing something for that?"

Lark held out his hand, showing his friends the red pads of his fingers. "I have to check my levels every hour. If I fall asleep for longer than that, wake me up."

"I think we should just take you to the hospital," Jace said.

"No. I just need to get on my feet again long enough to get home." He looked up at Sam. "Call my mom. The number should still be on your cell. Tell her how sick I am and ask her to send Clint."

Sam disappeared as Kade pulled Lark into his arms. "We'll get some fluid in you, but you need to try and eat something when you wake up," Kade said kissing him on the forehead.

He let his eyes slip shut. Sleep, that's all he wanted.

"Hey," Kade said with a soft nudge. "Wake up enough to drink some of this."

With Kade's help, Lark sat up enough to sip about half of the bottle of water. "That's all," he pronounced as he collapsed back against Kade's chest.

"When's the last time you checked your glucose levels?" Jace asked.

He felt so disoriented, he didn't even know how much time had passed. "Before I started meditating."

He heard Jace rifling around on Kade's desk before coming back with Lark's kit. "Here, give me your finger," Jace said.

He opened his eyes. Lark was coherent enough to know that wasn't a good idea. "No. Give it to me. You don't want to get my blood on you."

Lark heard Kade suck in a breath before cursing under his breath. "Give it to me," Kade demanded.

He felt a prick to his finger as Kade tested his levels. Once the monitor beeped, Kade held it up to his face. "What's your normal level?" Kade asked.

"It fluctuates between ninety-six and a hundred." Lark saw the reading on the small digital display. "I'll need a shot." He knew he was supposed to eat something thirty minutes after a shot, but his stomach rolled at the thought.

Lark gestured to the desk. "Jace, can you bring me that white pen looking thing on the desk?"

As Jace retrieved his insulin pen, Lark looked at Sam. "I think I need to try and eat a piece of bread." Sam nodded and took off.

With the pen in hand, Lark tried to pinch up an area of skin on his abdomen. He was losing weight at an alarming rate, even for him. He gave himself a shot and handed the pen back to Jace. "Thanks," he said settling back against Kade's chest.

He heard the phone ringing as his eyes slipped shut once again. He wasn't sure how long he slept before Kade was once again nudging him awake.

"Come on, baby. Your mom said you need to try and eat something," Kade said, kissing him.

Stretching, Lark opened his eyes. He was surprised how much better he felt. "How long have I been asleep?" he asked, noticing the room was empty except for him and his lover.

"Just forty minutes," Kade replied holding a piece of bread to Lark's lips.

Opening his mouth, Lark took a bite of the whole wheat bread. "I feel much better," he told Kade as he took another bite.

Before long, he'd finished off the last bite and gestured to the bottle of water. After finishing the water, he settled back into Kade's embrace. "Sorry about all that," he said. Kade was the one who was hurt, yet his man was actually taking care of him.

"Shhh," Kade said. "It's killing me to know I'm the one responsible for you being in this condition in the first place."

"No," Lark said, sitting up. "None of this is your fault. I knew the risks going into this. Besides, if I hadn't been trying to get to that beautiful cock of yours, we would've never wrecked in the first place."

Lark ran his hand down Kade's torso. He traced the chaos tattoo, still wondering how much pain a person had to be in to have that inked onto his skin forever. He watched as Kade's muscles rippled under his touch. Pushing the sheet down, Lark exposed Kade's hard cock.

"Just how much better are you feeling?" Kade asked with a wink.

Lark knew it was time when he read the 'Free Rides' tattoo just about Kade's cock. Without saying a word, he rose off the bed and went to his bag. Digging around the extra clothes he'd brought over, he at last found what he was looking for.

Walking back to bed, he held up the condom and bottle of lube. He gestured to Kade's tattoo. "Is that invitation open for just anyone?" he asked.

Kade's cheeks began to flush with apparent embarrassment. "I got that a long time ago, baby. You're the only one I want riding my cock from now on."

Kade looked him up and down for a few seconds. "Are you sure you're up to it? I've been without for so long, I'm not sure how gentle I can be."

Lark knelt beside Kade's hip and started opening the foil packet. "I've had nothing but silicone in my ass for damn near a year. Yeah, I think I'm up for a little ride."

He relished the feel of Kade's thick erection as he rolled the condom down its length. "Can I taste you first?" Lark asked, looking up into Kade's heavy lidded eyes.

Kade reached for the lube. "Swing that sweet ass around here and I'll get you ready while you torture me."

With a grin, Lark turned around to straddle Kade's body, head hovering above that heavenly piece of meat. Gripping the base of Kade's cock in his hands, Lark took his first lick. Even though the condom was flavoured, Lark would've much preferred to feel Kade's flesh under his tongue as he swirled it around the biggest crown he'd ever played with.

Lark moaned as Kade pressed his lubed fingers against his hole. "Feels good," he said before taking Kade's cock into his mouth.

Kade pressed one thick finger deep into Lark's ass. "I wish I could taste you," Kade grunted.

"Mmm, I'll remember the plastic wrap next time," Lark commented, coming up off Kade's length.

Kade started to chuckle as he introduced another finger. "Hell, you know more about this shit than I do."

Lark swallowed Kade's cock so he wouldn't have to say anything. Bo had taught him quite a bit in the time they were lovers. He pushed back into Kade's hand, needing his biker more than anything else at that moment. Pulling off, Lark begged, "Fuck me."

He felt Kade's cock twitch in his grasp at the invitation. Knowing his tough biker wouldn't be able to use his leg for a while yet, Lark turned to face him. His ass suspended above Kade's, Lark waited for permission to continue.

"You're in control for this one," Kade whispered, holding the base of his cock.

Lark slowly lowered himself until the fat crown pressed against his stretched hole. With a deep breath, he bore down as Kade thrust up. "Uhhhh," Lark moaned at the delicious invasion. He slowly impaled himself on his lover.

"Shit!" Kade exclaimed as Lark fully seated himself. "Been too long. I won't last," Kade mumbled as he started to move his hips under Lark's ass.

Bracing his hands on Kade's chest, Lark eased his body up and down, fucking himself on Kade's cock. Oh, damn, it was better than he ever imagined. He picked up his pace when he realised Kade was trying to buck up into him. "You sit still," he told his lover.

"Can't help it. I want more," Kade groaned.

"Give the leg another week or so to heal and I'll let you fuck me into oblivion, but for now, let me do all the work," Lark said, reaching up to Kade's nipple to pull at one of the tiny hoops.

That made Kade's chest break out in gooseflesh. With a smile, Lark readjusted his feet and started really riding his man. After a few minutes, his head started to spin a bit. He wasn't sure if it was the nausea returning or if he was weaker than he thought.

Not wanting to tell Kade, he decided to pull

out his next trick in hopes it would tip Kade over the edge. Reaching between his legs, Lark started stroking his cock. "See this? See how hard your dick is making me?"

He could tell by the flash of fire in Kade's eyes his plan was working. "Having you fill my ass is like a dream come true," Lark said. "You're the hottest fucker I've ever known. Just the thought of that big cock being inside my tight ass is enough to make me blow my load."

Kade released his hold on Lark's hips to pluck at his larger nipple rings. "You know what?" Lark asked his lover. "I'm gonna shoot all over your chest, and watch you lick it off."

Kade's eyes rounded, obviously forgetting that since he was already infected with the HIV virus, he didn't need to worry.

"Shoot towards my mouth," Kade finally said bracing himself into a half-sitting position.

Just the thought of watching Kade swallowing his essence was enough to push Lark over the edge. "Take it," he said as the first volley of seed flew through the air to land on Kade's cheek.

Kade quickly moved his head slightly and opened his mouth again, waiting for the next spurt. When it came, Kade caught it dead on. "Fuck," Lark moaned as he ground his ass down against Kade's balls. Two more shots and Lark saw Kade's torso contract as he filled the condom with cum.

Kade's body shivered as he emptied his seed. Lark was pulled down onto Kade's chest and given the mother of all kisses. The horizontal position seemed to help his dizziness, but not the overwhelming need to throw up.

Rolling to the side, Kade's flaccid cock slipped free of its warm home. "Sorry, I need to use the restroom," Lark said as he quickly fled from the room.

After throwing up the water and bread he'd eaten earlier, Lark brushed his teeth and re-entered the bedroom. "Sorry about that," he said as he joined Kade under the sheet.

Kade's brow rose as he wiped the sweat from Lark's forehead. "Did you just get sick again?"

He knew there was no use lying to his lover. "Yeah, but it wasn't as bad this time."

Kade pulled Lark closer to his chest. "Sleep. I'll wake you in an hour."

Lark nodded. "What time did Mom say Clint would be here?"

"Not until around midnight. You have plenty of time to rest before we need to go. Sam's already at the dorm packing up your clothes. Charlie said he'd store the rest of your stuff until we can get back."

With another nod, Lark kissed Kade's chest before dropping off to sleep.

Chapter Eleven

Aboard the small private jet, Lark watched Kade sleep. He felt guilty for not better preparing Kade before they reached the airport. Yeah, his mother had sent the plane for them, but it didn't actually belong to his family. It was the corporate jet for Sunrise Gardens.

Kade had stopped dead in his tracks as Clint, the pilot, met them at the small airport just outside of town. "Lark? Is there something you need to tell me?"

He'd shrugged and wrapped his arm tighter around Kade's torso. "I'm the same Lark I've always been. Trappings mean nothing to me, or my family." He'd looked up into Kade's eyes. "I hope they mean nothing to you as well."

Kade had let it drop there, but Lark knew they needed to talk before landing on the private airstrip in the compound.

A small glass of purple liquid was offered to him. "You need to drink this," Lars, his family's physician insisted.

"What it is?" he asked.

"It's Gator-Aid. With you unable to keep food down at the moment, you need it."

Knowing it would do no good to argue with the doctor, Lark took the glass. "I'll let you know when I'm finished."

One grey brow rose as Lars studied him. "Your mom is going to be upset at the amount of weight you've lost."

Lark chuckled. "Well I don't think I'm going to be able to gain it all back on the flight."

Rolling his eyes, Lars turned and walked back to the front of the plane.

Looking back down at his sleeping lover, Lark adjusted the cover. The small double bed in the rear of the cabin was the reason he'd decided to call for Clint. The plane hit a pocket of bad weather and began to bounce a little.

As he sipped his drink, Kade's eyes slowly opened. "How're you feeling?" Lark asked.

"Good, how 'bout you?"

Lark held up his sports drink. "Lars is trying to fatten me up."

Kade chuckled and ran his hand over Lark's chest. "I think he has his work cut out for him." Kade grasped the bottom of Lark's shirt and pulled it up to reveal the bruise. "I know I did this, and I'm sorry."

Lark shook his head and finished his glass so he could set it aside. Wrapping his arms around Kade, he kissed him. "Even the nurse at the hospital didn't blame you. I know you were just trying to protect me."

Kade ran his fingers through Lark's spiky hair. "Why did you do it? I know you told me you loved me, but why would you knowingly put yourself in danger like that?"

He'd known this talk was coming. He'd seen the questions in Kade's eyes several times since he'd first woken in the hospital. "You'll probably think I'm a sap, but let me finish before you say anything. Okay?"

Kade nodded.

"I grew up in an environment unlike most kids. I'm not saying it was bad, just different. There was a distinct difference between love and sex. You loved your family, but sex was something to be given and enjoyed at will. I've seen people give someone a blowjob instead of a handshake upon their first meeting."

Lark stopped and studied Kade's reaction before continuing. "I love my family, but when they sent me to the States it was a sort of culture shock. They hadn't prepared me for life outside the gated community where I'd been raised. My first week in the dorm, I was showering and saw a guy looking at me. I thought absolutely nothing of walking over and dropping to my knees in front of him. Moments after engulfing his cock in my mouth, I felt a steel hard fist against the side of my face."

"Who was he?" Kade broke in.

He could see the anger in his lover's eyes. "It doesn't matter, because it was my fault. It was my first lesson in life outside of Sunrise

Gardens. I kept pretty much to myself until Sam, but he wasn't even enough to drag me out of the shell I'd put myself in. Nope, it wasn't until I met you, that I knew I wanted to live again."

"Me?" Kade questioned.

"Yep, and it wasn't just because of your hot bod. Although, I must say, dayyyum. It was something I sensed the first time we met. I don't know if it's because you had closed yourself off or what, but I knew if we both opened ourselves, we could learn to love again."

With his hand to the back of Lark's head, Kade drew him down into a kiss. Lark had to admit he was momentarily disappointed with the brief kiss. Kade drew back. "I love you all the more for telling me that, but you still haven't explained why you've risked your life."

"Yes I have. I've told you every time I kissed you, sucked your cock, or let you become one with me. I love you, Kade. For the first time in my life, sex is more than sex. It means something. It's the way I can express my love for you without words."

Kade started to say something, but Lark kissed him into silence. "I risked my life because you *are* my life. If this medication doesn't work, and I end up positive, I'll deal with it. It's not nearly as worrisome as the thought of losing you."

"I don't know what to say. My own family disowned me when they found out. What is it about me that deserves someone like you?" Kade asked.

"Maybe you always deserved better than you gave yourself credit for. Could be you just finally opened yourself enough to accept it."

Kade pulled him down for another kiss. This one was what he'd been hoping for, all tongues and teeth. A clearing throat finally broke them apart. Looking over his shoulder, Lark smiled at Lars. "Yes?"

"We'll be landing soon. Clint would like for us to buckle up."

Lark nodded and gave Kade one last peck. "Lars, can you help me get Kade to a seat?"

"I'm perfectly capable of getting in my own seat. The leg is healing just fine," Kade grumbled sitting up.

Once they were buckled in, Lark squeezed Kade's hand. "There are a lot of very good looking men at the farm who will be more than happy to try and steal you away from me." He hadn't wanted to bring it up, but he had to know Kade would stay faithful.

Kade released Lark's hand and wrapped his arm around him instead. Pulling Lark closer, Kade kissed his temple. "I've had a lot of men in my life, and I know a jewel when I find one. Besides, look at this face." He gave Lark a scowl. "Does this look like someone you'd want to mess with? It's the face I plan on wearing whenever any of your old friends come to visit you."

Feeling much better, Lark traced the frown lines on the side of Kade's mouth with his tongue. "Bo's the only 'old friend' I have, and I think you'll like him."

"I doubt it," Kade said, capturing Lark's tongue between his teeth.

Clint came over the intercom and told them to prepare for landing. They'd already stopped off in Toronto to clear their way through Customs, so they would finally be landing at home.

Lark looked across Kade to gaze out the window. "This is Sunrise Gardens," he proclaimed.

"Holy fuck," Kade said.

Lark knew the farm was impressive from the air. Sunrise Gardens had grown from a small compound of organic farmers to one of the largest organic food producers in the world.

The plane touched down and rolled to a stop inside the one and only hanger. Lark unbuckled himself and stood. Holding out his hand, he helped Kade out of the seat. "Let's go meet the family."

* * * *

Lars picked up Kade's crutches, as Lark helped him off the plane. He still couldn't believe it. Sure he'd heard Lark mention the name of his parent's farm, but Kade had never imagined it was *the* Sunrise Gardens.

He smiled to himself. He wondered how many health food nuts would approve of the lifestyle that went on inside the compound.

The day was overcast as he stepped onto the tarmac. He watched as his lover ran to the group of people standing just off to the right.

"Mom, Dad," Lark yelled as he launched himself into their arms.

The sight of the family reunion brought tears to his eyes. What would it be like to have parents who accepted you, no matter what? He envied Lark down to the depths of his soul.

While still in their embrace, Lark turned his head back to Kade. "Come on and meet my folks."

Still a little afraid that Lark's parents would be angry with him for putting their son in danger, Kade retrieved his crutches from Lars and approached hesitantly.

Lark released his parents, and wrapped an arm around Kade. "Mom, Dad, this is Kade." Lark gave Kade a quick kiss. "Kade, I'd like to introduce you to Lynda and James Wilsher."

"Nice to meet you both," Kade said, reaching out to shake James' hand first.

The nice looking older man shook his head and pulled Kade into a hug. "We don't stand on formality here. Welcome to the family."

Kade was then passed off to Lynda. She cupped Kade's cheeks, studying him it seemed. "Yes, I can see what my son sees in you." Being small like Lark, Lynda wrapped her arms around Kade's stomach and hugged him.

Stepping back, she looked at the gentleman still standing to the side. "Meadowlark, Kade, I'd like you to meet Neil Bancroft."

Kade reached out and shook hands with Neil. There was something about him that was familiar but Kade couldn't place him. "Have we met before?" he finally asked.

"I don't believe so, unless you were in the Army?"

"Neil's a retired General," James added.

Shit. That's where Kade knew him from. He'd seen his pictures on the news and in magazine articles. "You're that Neil Bancroft?" He couldn't believe he was shaking hands with a war hero. He looked down at his lover. Lark was studying Neil closely.

After a slight nudge, Lark finally stuck his hand out. "Sir," he addressed the older man. Lark looked back at his parents. Kade wasn't sure what was going on, but his lover's spine was stiff as a board.

"Well, let's get back to the house." Lynda looked behind them. "Lars, why don't you ride with us? I'd like a current glucose reading on Meadowlark before you go."

"I'm feeling okay, mom," Lark put in.

Leading her son to the two extended golf carts, Kade smiled. A corporate jet, yet they drove electric vehicles.

It seemed James was reading his thoughts. "We rarely use the jet. That's why when Lark requested Clint, we knew he wasn't doing well."

Kade felt he needed to say something to the father of the man he loved. "I'm sorry, sir. I wouldn't blame you if you put my ass right back on that plane and had me shipped back to where I came from."

James shook his head and swung his arm around Kade's shoulders. "Life throws all of us curveballs from time to time. It's the way you catch them that matters."

As Kade climbed into the golf cart, he tried to figure out exactly what James had meant by that. Lark sat in the seat next to him and snuggled against his side. When Kade placed a kiss on his forehead, he pulled back. "You feel a little warm. How's your stomach doing?"

The look Lark gave him was all he needed to know. "How far is the house?" he asked Lynda.

"Just over the hill," she said as she pointed to the west.

He said nothing further to Lynda, but he bent down and whispered in Lark's ear. "Can you hold it until we get to the house, or do you need to stop?"

"I'll be okay," Lark answered burying his head against Kade's chest.

Kade prayed Lark was right. Hopefully once they got him into his childhood room, he'd relax enough to get better.

"Will you be staying at the house?" Kade asked Lars.

"I can, if I decide it's needed. Why?"

Kade tried to convey his worries without speaking them aloud for Lark and Lynda to hear. Lars must've picked up on them because he gave a slight nod.

There were moments Kade wondered if his lover would make it through the next day. Surely, these side effects couldn't continue for the full four weeks. Lark would be skin and bones within a week if he didn't start holding his food down.

"It's okay," Lark whispered.

Kade looked down. "I hope so, baby."

Chapter Twelve

Sitting on the side of the bed, Kade narrowed his eyes at the crutches leaning against the nightstand. He hated those damn things and so far had avoided using them. Looking down at a sleeping Lark, he felt his chest tighten. God he loved him.

Knowing his little man needed all the sleep he could get, Kade reached for his underwear, cut-off sweat pants and T-shirt. Getting his cock settled in the boxer briefs, he rolled his eyes. Damn he hated wearing underwear. He knew it was either that or take the chance of flashing someone.

After dressing, he stood and picked up the crutches. He was thankful Lark's family home was a ranch style. At least he wouldn't have a bunch of stairs to contend with.

Standing beside the bed, he bent and placed a soft kiss on Lark's pouty lips before heading out. He was already impressed with the set-up he'd seen so far. As they'd topped the hill earlier in the day, he was surprised to see an entire field of solar panels. Lark had chuckled at his surprised look and pointed towards the west. *We have wind generators over there. Mom and Dad practice what they preach. We're totally self sufficient here at Sunrise.*

"Amazing," Kade had said, more to himself than anyone else. No wonder Lark had been unprepared for the outside world.

Making his way down the hall, he heard voices coming from the kitchen.

"We have to tell him." Kade heard Lynda say.

"I know, but it worries me," James replied.

"Maybe I should get to know him a little first," Neil added.

Feeling like an intruder, Kade stood in the doorway. He knew he should probably leave, but he also could tell they were discussing the man he loved. Clearing his throat, Kade waited to be acknowledged.

James' gaze met his. "Come on in."

"I'm sorry if I'm interrupting. I couldn't sleep and didn't want to disturb Lark," Kade said making his way to the kitchen island. He was momentarily shocked to see Neil's arm around Lynda, but remembered what Lark had told him earlier.

"No problem," Lynda said. "Can I get you something to eat or drink?"

"A glass of water would be fine," he said sitting on a high stool and leaning his crutches against the island.

Before Lynda could break away from Neil's embrace, James stood. "I'll get it, sweetheart." As he passed, James stopped to give Lynda and Neil a quick kiss.

He saw Neil blush slightly as he looked back to Kade. "I'm sorry if this makes you uncomfortable. We've spent a lot of years apart. You don't realise what you have until it's gone." Neil looked down into Lynda's upturned face and kissed her.

Kade surprised himself as the words came tumbling out. "Nothing wrong with three people in love showing it."

"We're happy you feel that way. You'll see a little of everything at Sunrise. We're very open with love and affection. I hope Meadowlark's already prepared you," Lynda said.

"Yes, he has." There was a question he'd been dying to ask. "Would you mind me asking how you came up with Lark's name? I mean it's beautiful, and I can't imagine him with any other, but I'm curious."

Lynda looked at all three men before answering. "I grew up in the Midwest. I could lie and say it was the bird's melodious song that influenced our decision, but it goes a little deeper."

She looked at James. Kade watched as Neil's arms tightened, pulling Lynda even closer as James nodded. Looking back at Kade, she continued. "Did you know that most male Meadowlarks have two mates? In our case, it was the female that had two mates, but somehow we felt it fit."

Kade felt like he'd been punched in the stomach. Were they telling him...?

"Yes," Lynda said, reading his thoughts.

"I take it Lark doesn't know," he said. Kade felt like he was betraying his lover, finding out the truth before Lark did.

"We wanted to tell him in person," James added.

Kade couldn't help himself. Anger bubbled to the surface and came spewing out as he stood. "How could you have kept this from him for twenty-one years?"

He reached for his crutches, deciding it would be better to get the hell out of there before he said something he might regret. As he reached the door, he stopped and looked over his shoulder. "For people who claim to live open and honest lives, you three sure fucked up on this one. I've never seen a

Carol Lynne

man so in love with his parents. You'd better hope he's as forgiving as you think he is."

Kade turned the knob and stepped out onto the wide porch. His teeth ground together so hard, he was surprised they hadn't been reduced to powder.

Making his way down the four steps, he took off towards what looked like the town area of the compound. He was glad they hadn't tried to come after him. He was itching for a fight, and the last thing he needed was to get into one with Lark's parents.

Seeing what looked like a diner, Kade made his way inside. He needed to get off his crutches and think. He took a seat at the counter, and caught the waitress's eye. "Can I get a cup of coffee?"

The woman, Jan, her badge said, nodded. Bringing over the coffee pot, she turned his cup right side up and poured the hot black brew into it. "You must be Kade," she said.

"Yep." Kade hated to be rude, but small talk was the last thing on his mind.

"You're Kade?" A deep voice asked from behind Kade's back.

Kade felt the hairs on the back of his neck prickle. The way the guy had asked, Kade had a feeling he knew who it was. Turning around on his stool, he came face to face with one of the most attractive men he'd ever laid eyes on.

The guy stretched out a well muscled arm. "I'm Bo."

God help him, but Kade couldn't bring himself to shake Lark's ex-lover's hand. "I know who you are," Kade said.

Bo dropped his hand and looked around the room before looking back at Jan. "Can you give us a few minutes, honey?"

"Sure," Jan said and disappeared into the kitchen.

Upon inspection, Kade saw the two of them were now alone. Bo took a seat beside Kade, leaving an empty stool

224

between them. "If you know who I am, you know Meadowlark and I parted well. I didn't hurt him."

"Yep, I know that," Kade mumbled as he took a sip of coffee.

"So what's the problem?" Bo asked.

Looking at Bo, Kade narrowed his eyes. "Lark's mine," he growled.

He was once again thrown as a slight grin appeared on Bo's face. "Yes, I can see that."

Before Kade could say anything else, Bo continued. "I love Meadowlark, and I've never made a secret of that, but I've never been in love with him, nor him with me."

Taking another drink of his coffee, Kade felt like an ass. Bo was right, they both knew it. He wasn't used to being jealous and he wasn't sure how to handle these new feelings. "Fair enough," he finally said.

Bo stuck his hand out. "Hi, Kade, I'm Bo."

With a slight smile, Kade took Bo's hand. "Nice to meet you."

* * * *

After getting into Bo's golf cart, Kade was given a very thorough tour of Sunrise Gardens. He was still a little in awe of the place, when he saw Lark running towards them.

Bo pulled to a stop as Lark reached them and launched himself into Kade's arms. Knowing by the tears streaming down Lark's face he'd just had a talk with his parents, Kade looked back at Bo. "Is there somewhere Lark and I can be alone for awhile?"

Seeing Lark in distress seemed to be doing a number on Bo as well. "Yeah."

Kade lifted Lark into his lap as Bo took off. They were driven to a secluded grassy area beside a small pond. "Sorry, Meadowlark. I know this place holds a lot of memories, but I couldn't think of anywhere else."

Drying his eyes on the shoulder of Kade's T-shirt, Lark looked around. "It's okay, Bo. We'll be fine."

Bo climbed out of the vehicle. "I'm gonna leave this here and walk back. I think the two of you need it more than I do." Bo winked at Kade. "Take care of him."

"No doubt about it," Kade answered. He watched Bo's strong back as he walked back down the rutted path towards town.

Turning his attention back to the man in his arms, he kissed the top of Lark's head. "You wanna sit on the grass and tell me about it?"

Lark nodded and got off Kade's lap. They made their way to a shady spot and sat down. "Neil might be my dad," Lark blurted out.

Kade gave a slight nod and pulled Lark down against his chest. He had no idea what to say, so he waited for Lark to continue. "They were all living together when mom got pregnant. Neil had already signed up to go into the Army. I guess it's something he'd always wanted to do with his life. Unfortunately, a threesome with an illegitimate child didn't work into his plans, so he left them. Us."

Kade ran his hands down his lover's back, offering comfort as Lark worked things out himself.

"When he was sent overseas, Mom and Dad decided to move to Canada and make a fresh start for themselves." Lark shook his head. "I'm not really sure what happened, but they lost contact over the years. Neil happened to see a picture of them in a business magazine. That's when he decided to retire from the Army. I guess he showed up and my parents just took him in."

Lark stopped talking and sat up. "Just like that. They forgave him and moved him back into their lives without a thought as to what he'd done to them. And me."

Swallowing around the lump in his throat, Kade looked up at his lover. The sunlight streaming through the leaves caught Lark's hair and gave it a haloed effect. Yep, Lark was his angel, his salvation.

"I've made a hell of a lot of mistakes in my life," he started. "I hate the man I used to be, and the things I did to people who genuinely cared about me. For some unknown reason, you've been able to look past all that and love me anyway."

He pulled Lark back down into a kiss. "I'm sure Neil isn't proud of what he did, but he's here now trying to make up for it. You've got the biggest heart I know. Isn't there a little more room in it for Neil?"

Lark looked stunned. "You think I should forgive him? Just like that?"

"No, but I think you should allow yourself the opportunity to forgive him. It sucks that you didn't know about him, but from what I can tell, you had a great dad. I don't really think anyone expects you to call Neil, Dad, at least not until you're both ready for it."

Kade ran his fingers over the dark circles under Lark's eyes. "Neil's relationship with your parents is their business, not yours. All you have to ask yourself is if there's room to let him in."

"I love you," Lark said, capturing Kade's hand and bringing it to his lips. He gave Kade's palm a kiss before bestowing a sexy tongue bath over the callused skin. "Make love to me," Lark whispered.

Looking into Lark's face, Kade wanted nothing else in the world, but he knew better. "I can't do it the way I'd like to, because I don't have anything with me. Tonight, I promise."

"And every night after that?" Lark asked.

"Just try and stop me," Kade grinned and pulled Lark into another kiss. This one was more heated, as they both explored each other's warm depths. Kade's legs automatically spread as Lark climbed on top of him. "But for now, I'll make love to you my way."

When he felt his balls begin to draw up, Kade quickly pushed his sweats down before starting on Lark's zipper. When the two of them were finally skin to skin, Kade let out a moan.

With the size difference between the two of them, he knew he couldn't continue to kiss Lark if he wanted to feel their cocks rub together. Lark must've figured it out as well, because his lover began to lick his way down the tattoo on Kade's neck, stopping at his right nipple.

Rubbing back and forth against each other, Kade used one hand to torment the ring in Lark's nipple as he held the back of his lover's head. "Yes, baby, that's it," he groaned as Lark took the tiny hoop between his teeth and pulled.

Releasing his hold on Lark's piercing, Kade reached down and ran his hand down the cleft of his lover's ass. "God I want you," he panted, thrusting harder against Lark.

"Come for me," Lark said.

Like a trained puppy, Kade shot his seed seconds before Lark followed him over the edge. Scooting back up Kade's body, Lark kissed him, pushing his tongue in deep.

"Thank you."

"Hmmm, my pleasure," Kade mumbled.

After several minutes Kade's abdomen started to itch. Rolling Lark to the side, Kade took off his T-shirt and began cleaning himself.

"Hey, what about me?" Lark asked with a smile.

Bending down, Kade tossed his shirt to the side and began running his tongue through the thick creamy fluid. "You're mine," he said taking another swipe.

Once they were both taken care of, Kade asked Lark to help him up. "Are you ready to head back? It's almost time for me to take my pills."

"Sure," Lark said as he helped Kade to the cart. After getting Kade settled, Lark climbed in beside him. "Can I ask you something?"

"Of course," Kade answered.

"Where do you see yourself living in the future?"

Turning towards Lark, Kade cupped his lover's cheek. "Hopefully wherever you end up. Why?"

"I heard Jace talking about a place that I thought sounded interesting. Of course I'd have to finish school, but I was thinking maybe we could take a look when we drive back to Idaho."

Kade smiled. "I know exactly what town you're talking about, and yeah, I'd love to see it with my own eyes."

Chapter Thirteen

"Hey, Jace, what's going on?" Kade asked, answering his cell.

"Thought I'd let you know your Harley's good as new and parked in the garage."

"What? I thought I told you to sell it." Kade sat on the bench outside the medical clinic. He'd just completed his last physical therapy session.

"Yeah well, Lark called and offered to pay the insurance deductible. He said he'd never forgive himself if you sold the bike because of him."

Kade rubbed his ever expanding heart through his red T-shirt. "I thought I'd get an SUV or something when I got back. The bike is okay for me, but I won't take chances with Lark again."

"Kade, you love riding that damn thing. If you stop, you'll make Lark feel even worse about the accident. He already blames himself enough."

He decided to change the subject. "Well I'm good as new and Lark's finished his medication. He hit a few rough patches, but he seems to be doing well."

"So when are you coming home?" Jace asked.

"We're leaving in a couple of days, but we're driving back. Lark's folks bought him one of those new hybrid SUVs. I thought we might stop by that town in Wyoming you were telling me about."

"I'm jealous," Jace chuckled. "Promise you'll bring me back some cinnamon rolls and I'll even call Kyle and tell him you're coming."

Kade smiled. He knew Jace was addicted to those damn rolls and planned to get him a dozen all along. "Deal," he said. "We should be there in about four days. I want to take the trip a little slower than I normally would. Lark's not been sick, but he's lost a lot of weight and he's yet to get his strength back."

"Speaking of, where is your shadow?" Jace asked.

"He insisted on riding with Neil to check on the hemp harvest." Kade watched as Bo came out of the diner down the street. He'd found out later he was married to Jan, the waitress he'd seen his first day in town.

"So he's coming to terms with the fact that Neil may be his biological father?"

Kade thought briefly of the trouble Lark had had in the beginning trying to accept Neil's presence in his family home. "They've formed a tentative friendship. It'll take time for anything deeper to develop."

Bo spotted him and waved. "I gotta go, Jace. I'll see you in a week."

"Take care, buddy, and drive safe."

"Will do. I'll be transporting precious property on this trip." Kade hung up just as Bo stepped into the shade of the awning.

"You're looking good," Bo said reaching out a hand to Kade.

Kade smiled and welcomed the hand shake. He and Bo had spent quite a bit of time together over the last five weeks. With Lark sick in bed for much of the time, Bo had become a good friend.

He stood, still shaking Bo's hand. "I've been released. Seems I'm good as new," Kade said. "Care for a beer?"

Without a reply, Bo turned and started walking towards the small micro brewery on the farm. As they walked, Kade could tell something was on Bo's mind. He decided to wait until Bo felt comfortable enough to talk about it.

Walking into the lounge at the front of the brewery, Kade blinked several times to adjust his eyes to the dim lighting. Bo gestured to a small table in the corner. Kade knew it was out of character for Bo to ever sit in a corner. He was one of the most boisterous and friendly men Kade had ever met.

After taking their seats and ordering a beer, Kade waited.

"I want to make love to you," Bo finally blurted out.

Kade was shocked at first, but looking into Bo's eyes, he saw that the man was sincere in his request. Damn, a few years ago he would've been all over Bo. He could tell the man had a nice sized cock, with a body to match.

He suddenly realised he wasn't even tempted. "I'm flattered, but I'm in love with Lark."

"I'm not asking you to leave him. I just want to spend a couple of hours in your company," Bo replied.

Kade looked at the dark haired man across from him. He didn't know if he could explain what was going through his head and heart at the come-on, but he knew he needed to try.

"This may sound strange, but I really appreciate the offer. Probably not for the reason you think though. When I look at you, I see a gorgeous man I'd have jumped at the chance to fuck. Yet, strangely enough, I'm not even tempted this time. I've never been faithful to anyone in my life, and I'll admit, it had me worried. I guess I don't have to worry anymore. Lark's more than enough man for me."

Smiling, Bo reached across the table and took Kade's hand. "I'm happy for you. I don't know what it would be like to have one person satisfy all my cravings."

The look in Bo's eyes was so wistful. It tore at Kade's heart. "You love your wife?"

Bo's eyes filled with tears. "I love Jan. I'm just not sure I'm in love with her. Hell, maybe I've never been in love. I know I've never been tempted to fuck one and only one person for the rest of my life. I envy you."

Now it was Kade's turn to grip Bo's hand. "You deserve that, Bo. How does Jan feel about you?"

Bo shrugged his shoulders and took a drink of his beer. "She must feel the same. We do an awful lot of swapping. She just told me she was going out with the girls after work. That usually means I won't see her until she comes home to change for her next shift at the diner."

No matter how well he got to know the people of the town, he still didn't understand how they could just swap beds for the night. What he could tell by looking into the face of his new friend, was that it wasn't enough for Bo anymore.

"You should leave with us when we go," Kade stated. "Even if it's just a break away from Sunrise for a few weeks. There's a place I'd like to show you."

Bo's head jerked back a little in surprise. "Leave Jan and just take off?"

"Yeah, it's obvious neither of you are happy. At least not the way you should be. There's a town in Wyoming that I've been thinking about relocating to as soon as Lark finishes school. Cattle Valley was created for people like us. People looking for a place to fit in. Believe it or not, it's a GLBT community, from the Mayor on down."

"No way," Bo grinned and shook his head. "Why haven't I heard of it?"

"It's private. The town was started by a wealthy older man in memory of his son. Come on. Tell me you'll take the leap. Hell, maybe you'll check it out and decide Sunrise Gardens is the place you want to be, but I think you owe it to yourself to give Cattle Valley a shot."

"Why are you doing this? Why should you care where I end up?"

"Because if I didn't have Lark in my life, I'd probably be in bed with you right now," Kade grinned, "or at least in the bathroom shoving my cock deep in your throat."

"I'll give it some thought," Bo said.

"Hey, are you trying to scam on my man?" Lark asked, coming up behind Kade.

Kade turned and pushed back from the table enough for Lark to insinuate himself in Kade's lap. "Hey, baby," he said, giving Lark a deep kiss that lasted for several seconds. "You all done in the fields?"

"For now," Lark answered. He looked from Kade to Bo. "What's going on?"

Kade couldn't help himself. When Lark was near him, he had to touch his sweet body. He lifted the bottom of Lark's shirt and gently rubbed his stomach and chest as he answered his little man's questions.

"I'm trying to get Bo to leave with us. I want to show him Cattle Valley and I think he needs a break from Sunrise."

Lark's head tilted to the side as he seemed to study Bo. "Something going on, Bo?"

"No, not really. I've been telling Kade how much I envy what the two of you have." Bo looked at Kade. He could see the question in Bo's eyes and he gave a slight nod.

"I asked your lover to go to bed with me," Bo admitted. "He turned me down flat. Said you were the only man he needed or wanted. Then we got to talking and I think maybe Kade's right. Maybe it's time I allowed myself the chance to find that kind of love."

Lark leaned back more heavily against Kade's chest as he pushed his ass harder against Kade's raging hard-on. "I think you deserve that, Bo. You came to Sunrise because you were looking for a purpose. After all these years, I think you've just discovered it."

Kade watched as Bo's eyes tracked his hands as they slowly made their way down Lark's chest to rub against the thick ridge in his jeans. Kade gave Lark a kiss on the neck as he squeezed his lover's thick cock.

Bo quickly stood. Kade couldn't help but notice the small wet spot on the fly of Bo's pants. "I'm gonna go talk to Jan. I'll let you know in the morning what I've decided." He started to walk off but stopped. "You two are absolutely beautiful together." He gave them both a smile before leaving.

Moaning, Lark turned his head to the side and licked Kade's cheek. "I need you to come with me to the restroom."

"Hmmm," Kade said, undoing the top button of Lark's jeans. There were other people in the room, but this was Sunrise. Here, residents were used to others expressing themselves sexually. As bold as he was though, Kade didn't think he could fuck his lover in front of a room full of people.

With Lark's top button opened, he patted his lover's ass. "Let's go find a little more privacy."

Lark got up and pulled Kade to his feet. They walked arm in arm towards the men's restroom. Most public buildings in Sunrise had men's, women's and family's restrooms. You never really knew what you might walk into stepping into the men's room, so most parents took their children into the family one.

Kade was glad for the distinction. As soon as he had Lark alone, he began unzipping him. "Need you," Kade whispered.

While Lark finished getting his shoes and jeans off, Kade put four quarters into the condom machine on the restroom wall. He selected the heavily lubed condom and had it rolled on in no time.

Wrapping Lark in his embrace, Kade picked him up. Trapping his love between his chest and the wall, Kade wasted no time probing Lark's hole. He was pleased to find his lover still sufficiently stretched from their long session of love making earlier that morning. "Let me in," he moaned, as he pushed the head of his cock passed the first ring of muscles.

Lark gave a loud groan as his body seemed to suck Kade's cock in to the root. "Oh, fuck!" Kade exclaimed. Gripping the cheeks of Lark's ass in his hands, Kade started pumping in and out of his lover. He could feel Lark's body trying to hold him in place every time Kade withdrew his cock.

"Harder," Lark begged as he pulled up his shirt and began plucking at his nipples.

Kade moved his hands from Lark's ass to his waist as he took a step back. The new position had Lark's upper back and shoulders resting against the restroom wall. With a renewed sense of urgency, Kade pounded himself into Lark's hungry hole.

"Yesssss," Lark hissed as his cock erupted, throwing ropes of cum onto his hairless chest.

"Lemme taste," Kade said, looking at his lover's essence.

Lark ran his hand through the thick globs and held it to Kade's mouth. Kade felt his eyes roll back in his head at the strong taste of his lover's cum. The explosion of flavour inside his mouth pushed Kade over the edge into sheer bliss. He buried himself as deep as he could go and emptied his seed into the condom.

It was at such times he wished he'd never fucked anyone but the man in his arms. Knowing stupid choices in the past would forever hinder his love making with Lark, always caused him pause.

As his breathing slowed, Lark seemed to read his thoughts. "Don't. What we have together is too special for what ifs."

Kade pulled Lark back against his chest, moving his hands back down to the tiny ass he loved so much. "I love you," he said as he kissed Lark's soft, inviting lips. "Grow old with me and I'll love you more each day."

"Is that a promise?" Lark asked with a huge smile on his face.

Kade looked Lark in the eyes. "It's a vow."

Chapter Fourteen

After two days of driving, they pulled into Cattle Valley, Wyoming. It was still early, barely seven. They'd decided to drive the last leg of their journey straight through. Lark smiled to himself at the look on Bo's face. Although he'd finally agreed with Kade that it was time for him to take a break from the farm, Bo had been silent most of the trip west.

Now as Bo looked out the window, Lark could see the small town soaking into his pores. "Fucking fantastic," Bo mumbled loud enough for Lark to hear.

Lark had to agree. "Do they only let good-looking people live in this town?" he joked. Everywhere he looked as they drove into town were hot men. He glanced across the seat to Kade. "Cat got your tongue?" he asked.

Kade pulled the SUV in front of a row of shops. "I just can't get over this place. I mean, Jace told me, but it's better than I ever imagined. Look at that," he said pointing to the right. Two men were in an embrace right outside one of the stores. The taller of the two was wearing a police uniform, but from what little skin was showing, he looked more tattooed than Kade.

As they sat there, the two men started kissing. Lark felt his cock perk up in his jeans. Not that the guys themselves were turning him on, but damn they looked good together.

Kade noticed and reached across the console to brush his hand over Lark's erection. "Hot, isn't it?"

Lark finally tore his eyes away from the pair. "Any hotter and we'd have to find a secluded spot."

He looked in the backseat. "You okay, Bo?"

"Uh huh," he replied, eyes still glued to the frisky couple.

Opening his door, Kade chuckled. "Let's walk around a bit. I want to go in here and introduce myself to Kyle. Jace has given me strict orders to visit Brynn's Bakery upon arrival in town."

The three of them climbed out of the SUV. After a moment to stretch the kinks out, Lark joined Kade on the sidewalk. "Think there's a hotel in town?"

"I'd imagine, but I'm sure Kyle will be able to tell us." Kade pushed open the door to the bakery.

The smell of cinnamon hit Lark full force. "Oh, I'm gonna love it here."

Kade reached over and ran his hand down Lark's thin torso. "I think this is an excellent place to get you back to your normal weight. I only wish I didn't have to limit myself."

As they waited in line, Lark noticed the tall man in the cowboy hat checking Bo out. He gave his old lover a nudge to the ribs.

Bo looked down at him questioningly. Standing on tip toes, Lark whispered in Bo's ear. "I think you may already have an admirer."

One of Bo's black brows rose as he scanned the interior of the bakery. It was easy to tell when Bo spotted the cowboy. It was like his gaze was locked into place.

Well satisfied, Lark moved back into Kade's embrace. As he did, he couldn't help noticing the swelling of Bo's cock in his jeans. He couldn't tell how old the cowboy was, but he knew Bo looked much younger than his thirty-two years. He couldn't help but to wonder to himself how the cowboy would react to the news Bo was HIV positive if they ever managed to get together.

Bo started to walk towards the cowboy, but something strange happened. The cowboy turned, breaking eye contact and rushed out of the bakery. Lark looked from the strong retreating back to Bo. "Did you scare him away with your lustful good looks?" Lark asked, reaching a hand out to his friend.

"I'm not sure," Bo said. His voice was soft and Lark imagined a hint of insecurity in it.

Kade tugged on Lark's hand, bringing him back around. They stepped up to the counter. "Are you Kyle?"

Kyle smiled, showing his perfect white teeth. "You must be Kade. Jace said you'd be driving into town." They all introduced themselves, shaking hands.

Kyle looked at the line forming behind Kade and held up a finger. "Hold on, let me get my assistant to help these folks."

After disappearing into the back for several moments, he returned with a younger man in tow. "Care for a cup of coffee?"

"Sure," Kade replied.

Kyle motioned them back through the swinging door. At the far end of the bakery room, sat a small wooden table. Lark was glad Kade had already told him about Kyle being in a wheelchair. Not that he would've stared or anything, but it was better to be prepared.

He was surprised when Kyle stood and sat in one of the kitchen chairs. "Therapy," Kyle said, noticing the look on Lark's face. "I've got the best therapist in the world. Before long I won't need that damn chair at all."

"Congratulations," Lark said automatically.

Bo cleared his throat. "Excuse me, but do you have a restroom I could use?"

Kyle pointed to the back of the room. "There's a little hallway. On the right is the elevator and on the left is the restroom."

"Thanks," Bo said and walked in that direction.

As soon as Bo was out of earshot, Lark couldn't help himself. "Can you tell me who that good-looking cowboy in the big black hat was who was in here earlier?"

"I didn't see him, but it sounds an awful lot like Rance Benning. Why? Do you follow the rodeo circuit?"

"No," Lark said and gestured towards the restroom. "There seemed to be a mutual attraction between him and Bo, but when Bo tried to walk over to introduce himself, the fella practically ran out the door."

Pouring four cups of coffee, Kyle nodded. "Yep, it was definitely Rance then. He doesn't talk much unless it's about business. Doesn't socialise much at all. Oh, I've seen him have a beer a time or two at Brewster's, but that's it."

Kyle pointed towards a baker's tray of freshly frosted cinnamon rolls. "Care for a bite?"

Lark licked his lips. He still had questions about the good-looking cowboy, but decided to drop it. They were only in town for a couple of days and he didn't need to gain the reputation as a busy body.

Chuckling, Kade rose at Kyle's instructions and placed several of the rolls onto a plate. He brought them back to the table, and Lark wasted no time in snagging one. His first bite had him moaning. "Oh, oh, I'm in love."

Kade bent and nipped Lark's shoulder. "Watch it. I'd hate to get jealous of a lump of dough."

Looking at Kade, Lark purposely coated his lips with frosting and leaned up for a kiss. Kade's tongue swept over Lark's lips, cleaning the frosting. "Mmm, well, I guess if we're going to get involved in a threesome…"

Kyle and Bo started laughing. As Lark pulled a small amount of the delectable cinnamon roll off and fed it to his man, he heard Bo ask about a hotel.

"We've got the bed and breakfast, but I'm afraid they're booked up right now. If you all are planning to stay in town for a couple of days, I'd be happy to let you stay upstairs. It only has the one bedroom, but it's got a pretty decent couch."

"That would be very nice of you," Bo said. "What do you guys think?"

With his finger still embedded in Kade's mouth, Lark nodded. "If you don't mind. I'd hate to have to drive all the way to Sheridan. My hungry lover here has visions of settling down in Cattle Valley after I graduate. It would be nice to get a better feel of the town before making any decisions."

"Well then it's settled."

* * * *

Two mornings later, Lark was coming down from an unbelievable orgasm, when Kade started kissing him again. "Go easy on me, love. I'm not up to full strength yet," he joked.

Kade grinned. "Well then, you'll have to eat twice as many rolls for breakfast."

Lark laid his head on Kade's tattooed shoulder. "I almost hate to leave this place."

"We'll be back," Kade said.

"I think Bo wants to stay. He told me he was going to apply for a job at the software company here in town."

Lark had worried a little about his friend over the past several days. Ever since seeing that studly cowboy, he'd been a little withdrawn.

"Hey," Kade said tilting Lark's chin up. "Something wrong?"

"No, not really." He closed the distance and kissed Kade. "Will you ask Tony for your job back once we get home?"

"Yeah, probably. With only another year before you graduate, I'd hate to get a different job only to quit next spring."

They kissed for several long leisurely moments. "Do you mind living with a poor, working man?" Kade asked.

He'd said it like a joke, but Lark knew there was fear behind his words. Yeah, Lark's family was wealthy, and he had a large sum of money in trust, but money meant nothing to him, it never had. *Wait a minute.* "Did you say living with?"

Kade smiled. "Yeah, I kind of thought we could get a small apartment close to the university. That is, if you're interested."

Lark climbed on top of Kade's powerful nude body and began kissing the tattoo on his lover's chest. "Does that mean I've totally melted the ice around this big heart of yours?"

Kade thrust up against Lark. "It melted to a puddle the first time you kissed me."

About the Author

An avid reader for years, one day Carol Lynne decided to write her own brand of erotic romance. Carol juggles between being a full-time mother and a full-time writer. These days, you can usually find Carol either cleaning jelly out of the carpet or nestled in her favourite chair writing steamy love scenes.

Carol loves to hear from readers. You can find her contact information, website details and author profile page at http://www.total-e-bound.com

Total-E-Bound Publishing

www.total-e-bound.com

Take a look at our exciting range of literagasmic™
erotic romance titles and discover pure quality
at Total-E-Bound.